Southern Gothic

A MAX PORTER PARANORMAL-MYSTERY

Stuart Jaffe

Southern Gothic is a work of fiction. Names, characters, places, and incidents either are the product of the author's imagination or are used fictitiously, and any resemblance to any persons, living or dead, business establishments, events, or locales is entirely coincidental.

SOUTHERN GOTHIC

Cover art by Jeff Dekal

ISBN 13: 978-1-7337308-6-0

First Edition: January, 2015
First Hardcover Edition: January, 2024

For Glory and Gabe
again and always

Also by Stuart Jaffe

Max Porter Paranormal Mysteries
- Southern Bound
- Southern Charm
- Southern Belle
- Southern Gothic
- Southern Haunts
- Southern Curses
- Southern Rites
- Southern Craft
- Southern Spirit
- Southern Flames
- Southern Fury
- Southern Souls
- Southern Blood
- Southern Graves
- Southern Dead
- Southern Hexes
- Southern Hart

Nathan K Thrillers
- Immortal Killers
- Killing Machine
- The Cardinal
- Yukon Massacre
- The First Battle
- Immortal Darkness
- A Spy for Eternity
- Prisoner
- Desert Takedown
- Lone Star Standoff
- The Puppeteer
- Blowback
- Prime

The Ridnight Mysteries
- The Water Blade
- The Waters of Taladoro
- Waterfire

The Parallel Society

The Infinity Caverns
Book on the Isle
Rift Angel
Lost Time
Pages of Glass
The Bold Warrior
City of Infinity

The Malja Chronicles

The Way of the Black Beast
The Way of the Sword and Gun
The Way of the Brother Gods
The Way of the Blade
The Way of the Power
The Way of the Soul

Gillian Boone novels

A Glimpse of Her Soul
Pathway to Spirit

Stand Alone Novels

After The Crash
Real Magic
Founders

Short Story Collection

10 Bits of My Brain
10 More Bits of My Brain
The Bluesman
The Marshall Drummond Case Files: Cabinet 1
The Marshall Drummond Case Files: Cabinet 2
The Marshall Drummond Case Files: Cabinet 3

Non-Fiction

How to Write Magical Words: A Writer's Companion
For more information, please visit ***www.stuartjaffe.com***

Acknowledgements

It has been written endless times that no book is created alone. It's quite true. This time around I give my deep thanks to Jeff Dekal, for delivering on a wonderful cover; Mom and Dan, for visiting and then asking that I take you around Winston-Salem on a Max Porter tour (some of the locations in this volume came from that day); all of my social media followers for constantly keeping me driven; to my wife and son, the best motivators of all; and of course to you, my readers. Without you, these stories don't amount to much more than my ramblings. Thanks.

Southern Gothic

Chapter 1

MAX PORTER DID NOT LIKE THE POLICE. If a cop drove behind him, even if he was innocent of any wrongdoing, his stomach would lurch and his adrenaline would pump hard. Being an unofficial detective for the last few years had not altered his attitude. He knew the police were good to have around when trouble turned against him, but too often the kind of trouble that involved him — ghosts, witches, curses — was the kind of thing that got one arrested and locked up in a padded cell. So when he pulled up to the enormous Baxter House, when he saw the numerous flashing red-and-blues along with yellow police tape blocking off the house, he tried to remain calm and reminded himself that he had done nothing wrong. Not recently, at least.

The house did little to ease his mind. Located in one of the most affluent sections of Winston-Salem, the building sat on a full acre right off Buena Vista Road. Surrounded by million-dollar homes, Baxter House lacked all the charm of its neighbors. Whereas most of the mansions on the street were gleaming white affairs with manicured lawns and a distinctly Southern flair, Baxter House stood like a stark, short castle intended to be situated on a grassy field in the cold rains of Great Britain. The overcast, winter afternoon completed the gloomy atmosphere.

Only thing missing is a bunch of gargoyles, Max thought.

As he approached an officer standing by the yellow tape, a gust of wind cut across the yard. He winced and turned his head away. Winter in North Carolina never had the deep snows that Michigan produced, rarely had any snow at all, but the winds bit sharp and vigorous.

The officer stomped his feet on the ground as he paced along the line of tape. Max wondered how much trouble was barreling down on him. Life had been hard enough lately without dancing a tango with the cops.

The officer lifted a gloved hand, but Max pointed at the house. "I'm Max Porter. I was told to come here by Detective Robson."

"Rolson. With an 'L'." The officer lifted the tape as Max ducked under. "Go on inside."

Heavy double-doors stood open at the front, but little heat came out. Another officer stood guard, a cup of coffee in his hands. When Max explained why he was there, the officer led him into the house, clearly relieved to be getting inside. The foyer was big enough to be a master bedroom in most homes. Dark woods and a thick, Turkish floor rug pressed in from all sides. A long staircase followed the walls up to the second floor.

The officer went off to the right and weaved his way from one room to the next. They passed through an immaculate kitchen where two more officers leaned against a marble counter and sipped coffee. The officer pointed ahead and then left.

Max went three more steps before an overweight, black man with a hooked nose and a stark white horseshoe of hair running around his head walked straight toward Max.

"You with the Coroner's Office?" he asked.

Max said, "No. Are you Detective Rolson?"

The man laughed, revealing a discolored yellow tooth. "I'm with the Crime Scene Unit. Rolson's in there."

Just ahead, more crime scene techs took photos and bagged evidence. Max entered the main source of activity — the study.

Volumes upon volumes of tomes lined the walls from floor to ceiling. A beautiful mahogany desk occupied the back of the study and a lovely fireplace filled the area behind the desk. Off to the right, a large arched window looked out to the back acreage. If not for the dead body face down on the floor, the study would have been the envy of anybody who loved books and learning.

A stocky man with thin, blond hair and a sharp nose turned to Max. He wore a faded red sweater under his suit coat that made him look more like a befuddled professor rather than a homicide detective.

Smiling, he offered his hand. "Mr. Porter? I'm Detective Eric Rolson. Thank you for coming."

"Of course. But I have to say, I'm not quite sure why I'm here. I've never been to this house before. How can I help you?" This was the real source of his nerves. Being called to a murder scene meant either Max was a suspect or the police needed his unique qualifications to aid them. Since they had never before called upon his ability to see a ghost nor his wife's ability to see all ghosts, he figured he was a suspect.

Rolson's smile never wavered. "The victim is Sebastian Freeman."

"Oh, crap." Until that moment, Max had not looked too closely at the dead man. He had seen dead people before and found the morbid fascination wore off quickly. But now, he saw that indeed, the man was Sebastian Freeman. A tall, black fellow with a thin but strong body.

"I'll take it that means you know the man."

Max's stomach flipped twice as he nodded. "He was my client. My only client."

"We found your business card on the victim's body. That's why we called you. Figured you might be able to help us with a few details."

"Sure. Of course."

"What exactly were you doing for Mr. Freeman?"

"Ancestry. I'm a researcher. He hired me to trace his family back."

"My wife's into all that, too. Uses a website for it. Found out my family goes all the way back to a little town in Switzerland called Binn. Fascinating stuff. So, Mr. Freeman hired you for research?"

"That's right."

"You do this kind of thing regularly? Ancestry?"

"Not regularly enough." Max could hear his wife, Sandra, warning him — *Careful with the sarcasm. Just answer the man directly.*

"I guess it's hard to get people to pay you for that kind of work. I mean, can't they all do like my wife and use the Internet?"

"Those sites are great for locating census records, names, dates, that kind of thing. In fact, I use them, too, in order to get the basics. But when you want a more in-depth look into your past, the kind of thing that not only finds names and dates but actual stories, maybe even a lost diary or something like that, well, that's where I come in."

"And Mr. Freeman paid you for that kind of *in-depth* search?"

"Yup. Particularly, he wanted me to search for any ancestors he had that might have been slaves. All his efforts to locate where he came from stopped around the end of the Civil War, so he wanted me to see if I could do anything better, find anyone further back."

"Did you?"

"Not yet. I'd only been working on it for a couple days."

"Okay. When was the last time you saw Mr. Freeman?"

"Two days ago, I guess. We spoke on the phone last night, though. He wanted to know how far I had gotten. Really pushy about it, too."

"Did he sound worried? Did he maybe mention anybody threatening him?"

"No. Just that he wanted the answer as soon as possible."

Rolson pulled out an old flip notepad and jotted down a few words. It reminded Max of Marshall Drummond — his ghost partner who had been a detective in the 1940s. Where was he, anyway? Ever since the old office had been destroyed, Drummond had become free to go wherever he wanted, but he spent most of his time driving Max crazy. Now, when having a ghost detective would be useful, the guy was nowhere in sight.

Rolson tapped his notepad. "Was Mr. Freeman timely in paying you or did he complain about money problems?"

"He paid a small fee at the start — two hundred dollars —

and the rest would come when I finished. I guess I won't be getting paid." Max tried not to sour his expression, tried not to sound as crestfallen as he felt, but they sorely needed that money.

"Almost done here. Just a few more questions. Tell me, do you know why Mr. Freeman was here at the Baxter House?"

Max shook his head. "I know nothing about this place. Never seen it before. Heck, I've never really had reason to come to this part of town before. Who lives here?"

"Nobody."

Max gestured to all the books and furniture. "Somebody's been living here."

"Baxter House is one of the cities little eccentricities. This place has stayed empty for decades, but it's kept clean and running anyway."

"Why?"

Rolson shrugged. "Rich people. They get nutty with their wills. Give all their money to a family pet, make strange requests for their funerals, that kind of thing. When Cal Baxter died, I think it was in the 1920s or 30s, he must've had one whopper of a will."

"Hey," a deep, muffled voice called out, "what's going on here?"

It took Max an extra second to realize nobody reacted to the voice, and that meant nobody had heard it but him — and *that* meant Drummond had finally decided to show up. The dead detective slipped through an outer wall and gave Max a short wave. He wore the classic trench coat he had died in, complete with Fedora, and all the gruff, chiseled features of a man who had lived a rough life. Yet despite his unpleasant encounters with the living and the dead, Marshall Drummond maintained a positive outlook on his existence, one that often girded Max into positive actions for himself.

Rolson continued, "But you're saying you've never been to this house before?"

"Never."

"This looks bad," Drummond said, and Max deflated. "Hey,

isn't that dead guy the colored fellow who hired you?"

Max bit back the urge to correct Drummond's backwards choice of words. Rolson still stood in front of him and would certainly find it strange if Max started talking to empty air.

Rolson asked, "Any idea why Mr. Freeman was here? He ever mention this place?"

"No. He gave me what he knew about his family, which wasn't much, and asked me to start looking. Didn't really tell me anything else, and I didn't ask. I was looking into the past for him, not the present."

Drummond took a quick tour of the study. "Looks like I missed all the fun. Now that I'm no longer stuck tied to the office, I'm finding there's an even larger ghost world out there. I mean, I've been in the Other — you remember that's what we call it? — but I had no idea just how big that place is. And the women. Holy mackerel. Let's just say that when the mortal coil is shuffled off, so are a lot of inhibitions. Don't get me wrong — it ain't anything close to as good as when I was alive, but it ain't half-bad either."

Trying to focus both Drummond and his own mind, Max looked at Detective Rolson and said, "I'm sorry I can't help you more. Do you have any idea who killed him?"

Rolson pocketed his notepad. "We just found the body. Give us a little time."

"Of course. Sorry."

Drummond hovered over Sebastian's corpse. "That's strange. No blood on the floor. No blatantly visible wounds. How was this guy killed?"

The muscles in Max's neck relaxed a bit as he heard Drummond's investigative mind take over. Gesturing to the body, he repeated the question to Rolson.

"You are an impatient man." Rolson made no attempt to hide the growl in his voice. "I already said we just got here. How could I know the cause of death when we haven't even finished processing the crime scene?"

"I meant no offense. I only asked because I don't see any blood or wounds or anything."

"Well, you wouldn't. He wasn't shot or stabbed. We'll probably find evidence of strangulation or maybe he had heart attack and there's no homicide at all. I won't know officially until the M.E. gives her report. Unofficially, however ..." Rolson leaned in close to Max and whispered. "... you can shut up and go home."

Drummond grunted. "Rude little prick."

Max forced a gentle smile. "I apologize if I overstepped my place in all this. I've never stood in a crime scene like this before. It's all a bit overwhelming."

Rolson puffed up a little and brushed at his jacket. "Oh, well, of course. This can be a bit exciting for the novice, I guess. But it isn't like you see on the cop shows. For a case like this, we won't get answers super-fast. Nobody's going to put the rush job here."

"Why? This isn't like New York City where murders happen probably every day. I can't imagine you have that many to deal with in Winston-Salem."

Rolson raised an eyebrow. "More than you'd believe. Too many, as far as I'm concerned."

Drummond had drifted over to the desk. "Keep him talking. I'm working as fast as I can."

It took Max a huge effort to keep his eyes on Rolson. He didn't know what Drummond's *work* consisted of, and he didn't want to know. Putting out his hand for a shake, he said, "Well, Detective, I guess that's it. I came, I saw, I answered questions. I suppose none of this has anything to do with me anymore."

"What are you doing?" Drummond soared over next to Rolson. "Your client was murdered. You can't walk away from that. Besides, you haven't had an interesting case in ages. This is a murder. That's big."

"One second," Rolson said, holding up his index finger. "I have another question for you. I'll be right back." He walked out of the room with a firm clip to his step.

Drummond got right in front of Max. "Listen to me. I know you. You aren't going to pretend this didn't happen. You can't."

In a harsh whisper, Max said, "Nobody's paying us to look into this murder, and in case you haven't noticed, money's been a bit of a problem. So while I'm sorry for Sebastian, I can't really help him either. Especially since he's dead."

"Have you learned nothing since we've met? Do you listen to anything I tell you?"

"I try not to."

"You better listen this time because your life is probably in danger." Drummond passed over the corpse. "This man is dead only a short time after hiring you to start digging into his past. That doesn't strike you as an important sequence of events?"

"There's no reason to think that the two are connected."

"Oh, Max, don't be naive. If I've taught you anything, it should be that when it comes to crime, there are no coincidences. Not like this, at least." Drummond looked in his coat pocket and frowned. Joshua Leed, a highly educated witch hunter, who had been reduced to a ghostly glob which Drummond carried around, still managed to talk with the old detective, though Max could not hear a word — Drummond was the only ghost on Max's otherworldly radar.

A moment later, Drummond slid over to the desk. "You don't want to believe me, okay. I'm telling you my gut knows there's something wrong here and that you might be in danger. Or maybe even Sandra. Leed agrees."

"Are you really going to go after my wife with this?"

"Stop being a brat, come over here, and grab these papers before the copper comes back."

Max stomped over to the desk, his eyes blazing. "I'm not going to steal evidence because of your gut-feeling when you don't even have a gut anymore."

But even as Max spoke, his fingers brushed the papers. He could deny Drummond for all eternity but that wouldn't change the nagging in the back of his head — the voice that reminded him how Drummond knew this line of work too well, that he would never suggest stealing like this unless it was important, that Drummond cared deeply for Sandra and maybe even for Max, too. That voice also pointed out that Max's gut had been sharing Drummond's uneasy feelings about this crime scene.

With a quick glance at the door, Max grabbed the papers, folded them once, and shoved them into his pocket.

Great, Max thought. *Now, I'm a thief.*

Chapter 2

DURING THE ENTIRE DRIVE HOME, Max did not utter a word. The stolen papers weighed down his pocket a little and his conscience a lot. When Drummond realized his partner would not be speaking, he settled in the back seat and talked softly with Leed.

Twenty minutes later, Max pulled off Peters Creek Parkway onto a gravel road that led to a rundown trailer park — fourteen trailers lined up in three rows. Next door, the heavy fumes of a Marathon gas station polluted the air. Across the street and a down a little, a McDonald's did the same.

Max slammed his car door shut and trudged over to his trailer. Ever since the resurrection of Tucker Hull, life for the Porters had become difficult. They lost their home, their business, everything. But Sandra refused to be run off with tail tucked. Much of the time, her strength kept Max going. Even when they learned that Forsyth County mysteriously annexed certain properties from neighboring Davidson County with the end result that Max's trailer now sat in the higher tax-bracketed Forsyth — even when that happened, and he knew in his heart that the Hull family had engineered the unfortunate turn, seeing Sandra's jaw jut out and her fists clenched inflated his confidence. She would not let them break her or Max, so Max had to be strong, too.

Except when Max entered their trailer, he had to stop and observe the squalor of their lives — a torn couch, a chipped table for two, rusting appliances, a closet-sized bathroom, stained carpets, and a grimy odor that coated his clothes and skin. Was this really what they fought for? And now Drummond wanted Max to jump into a mess involving a murder. Probably to stave off the old ghost's boredom. Sure, he said that trouble approached, but so what if it did? They had so little left, they had nearly reached the point of *nothing to lose.*

Drummond entered through a wall. "I know that look. You're upset. Let me tell you something."

"No." Max pulled the stolen papers from his pocket and tossed them in the trash. "We've got one of the wealthiest families in all of North Carolina gunning for us, which is bad enough, but then add to that the fact that this family is led by a man dead since the 1700s and, oh yes, did I mention that they have used witches and magic for centuries? And you think I should be concerned over the murder of some guy I hardly knew who only wanted to find out about his family? Really?"

"Something inside you knows I'm right. Otherwise, you wouldn't have taken those papers."

"Thanks for that, too. I've committed a serious crime, stealing evidence, so now I can improve my life by going off to jail. I'm sure Sandra would love visiting me, only talking through a phone, seeing me bruised and beaten — you know I'm not tough enough to stand my ground in jail. They'll rip me apart."

"Max, please, you're acting hysterical."

"I am not going to get involved in this."

A car pulled up and backfired — Sandra. They had needed a second car but couldn't afford anything but a used piece of junk that clearly had been in more than one accident. Max watched from the dirty window as she turned off the car and gathered her things together. He dashed the three steps it took to get to the trash and fished out the stolen papers.

"Over here," Drummond said, indicating a torn piece of carpet near the back wall.

Max shoved the paper under and placed a pillow over the ripped carpet. With a harsh look, he pointed a finger right at Drummond's face. "Not a word."

The door opened and in walked Max's wife. Sandra still could take his heart away. Even in the hard times they suffered through, looking at her shapely figure and bright smile gave him hope.

Max wrapped his arms around her and planted a big kiss on her mouth. She smiled playfully. "Now that's the kind of welcome home I like." Hearing her own words, Sandra frowned. "Wait a minute. Why are you home? Shouldn't you be researching some family history?"

"I have some bad news about that. My client is dead."

"What?"

"I'm hoping it was an accident or natural causes."

Drummond stretched his arms over his head and groaned. "That colored boy was murdered and you know it."

With an impatient sigh, Max said, "He wasn't a *boy* and I swear if you use the word *colored* again, I'm going to end our partnership."

"What did I do?"

"Don't act all innocent. You've been haunting this world for decades. You know all about the Civil Rights Movement, about the changes in this world, and you know that the way you thought back when you were alive was wrong. So start checking that your mouth is synced up with the times. We've got enough problems without having to deal with Southern bigotry."

"Now you listen here —"

"Gentleman," Sandra said with an easing tone. "Let's not argue about prejudices that neither of you have. Drummond, kindly update your vernacular so that you speak less offensively in this modern world. Max, stop taking the bait for a fight simply because you and Drummond are feeling ornery. And one of you, tell me what the hell happened today? Your client was murdered?"

Max slumped into the kitchen chair. Sitting wedged between the sink and their only table, Max explained the events of the day. He never mentioned the papers he stole nor that he had them stashed underneath the carpet, but otherwise, he provided every detail as best as he could recall.

When he finished, Sandra pounded her fist against the counter with one hard strike. "It's not fair. We can't even get a break on a simple damn family research job."

"I'll get some other work. Don't worry. It'll be okay."

"No, it won't. How are we going to survive if Hull kills off every client you get?"

"We don't know it was Hull. We don't even know if it was murder."

Sandra dropped her purse on the table. Its stitching had started to unravel, and she flicked the loose, limp strands. "I can't support us both working part-time at a bakery, and they won't give me any more hours."

"It's not your job to support us. We do it together."

"Not when you have no clients."

Drummond tipped his hat and lowered his head. "I think I should be going for a bit of a stroll. See you later." Max opened his mouth to utter a word of protest, he figured having the ghost's support might help in this fight, but before he could speak, Drummond floated away.

Max turned toward Sandra. "We've been through tough times before, and they say the economy is getting better. I'm sure more clients will come our way."

"Stop that. You're always playing the part of Mister Positive when I'm pissed, but I know deep down you're angry and worried about all of this."

"Of course. We've got plenty to be angry and worried about. That doesn't mean we have to give up, and we certainly don't have to fight about it. It's not like this is my fault."

Sandra's eyes flared. "Don't you start blaming me."

"I didn't —"

"Just because I'm the one who had the guts to tell Tucker Hull to go back to the hell he came from, doesn't mean this is all my fault. Or would you have rather we ran away from North Carolina and simply prayed that a psychopathic zombie with a witch fetish would forget about us? You really think that would've worked? The Hulls never forget. Look at all of your big cases down here. Every one of them that involved the Hulls, and that's almost all of them, involved old scores they were still trying to settle. You really think they'd let us go? After you held them off of us by threatening to expose them? You really think that?"

When Max sensed that she had vented the last of the moment's anger, he smiled. "When I said it wasn't my fault, I meant my client's murder. That's it."

Sandra stood next to the refrigerator, suddenly finding great interest in the dent from where the previous owner had kicked it. "Oh," she said. "Sorry."

Her bottom lip quivered and as her tears fell, Max swooped her up in his arms and stroked her hair. "I don't blame you for any of this. When you sent word to the Hulls that we weren't going to run, I was so proud of you. And I still am."

Sniffling, she said, "I know. I do. I'm just sick of things not going our way. Ever. It seems like every time we're so close to building a stable life, some catastrophe happens to knock us back down. I swear all of those catastrophes have the name Hull attached somewhere along the line."

"Hey, don't worry so much. We've still got each other. And this lovely home."

With a chuckle, she stepped away and grabbed a tissue. "That we do. When they get this away from us, we can live out of the car."

"That's right. The Fall is almost done, but we can drive further South if the ice storms get too bad. Otherwise, the weather here is fine. Who needs a house?"

"I'll tell you, seriously, it's hard not to see the Hulls hands in everything bad. Even when I was asking for more hours, the way Cheryl hesitated before saying she couldn't do it — I swear she needs the help, and all I could think was that Hull got to her, too."

Max nodded. "I feel it, too. Driving up to the crime scene today, I saw those cops, and I couldn't really put it into words until now, but yeah — I think I had that same suspicion. I didn't even know what had happened yet, but on some deep, subconscious level, all I could think was that the Hulls were about to screw up my life again."

Max thought about the papers under the carpet. He had yet to look at them, and he wondered if the letterhead would be a big blue H with a little door on the one leg.

Sandra hugged Max. "Let's promise not to talk about the Hulls anymore. At least, not anymore tonight."

"Okay. Deal."

"You know, Drummond ran off because we were fighting."

"Yeah, I saw him go."

"That means he's not here to bother us. Not for a while. We're all alone."

Max felt his lips curl upward. "Now that is a much better way to spend our time than fighting."

Sandra pressed her mouth against his, and he wasted no time reaching for her bottom. He felt a bit like a teenager whose parents had stepped out. The kisses between them had that urgency, that strength and desire which accompanied making up as well as the fear of getting caught.

He heard a car pull up outside but did his best to ignore it. He heard the car door shut but dismissed it as a neighbor stopping home early. His hand reached up Sandra, but they both stopped as they heard three sharp knocks on their door.

"Damn," he muttered.

Sandra kissed the tip of his nose. "Raincheck?"

"You need to ask?"

With a wink, she opened the door. A tall, stark lady dressed in an expensive business suit stepped in. She extended her hand, and with a clipped tone, she said, "Good day. I'm Cecily Hull."

Chapter 3

IF MAX HAD BEEN ASKED all the numerous ways his day could have gotten worse, he would never have dreamed up this. Cecily Hull stood in their trailer with a disgusted twist to her mouth as she examined the poor conditions. She had short, blonde hair styled with sharp ends and a close buzz in the back — a rather intimidating look when coupled with her pale skin and grim eyes. One might assume she had been dressed for a funeral, except Max's gut told him this was her standard appearance.

She stood still with her hand out, and Max finally realized Sandra had no intention of being polite. Why should she? A few years ago, Max would have agreed with Sandra's attitude and probably took a step further. But he knew better now. This woman had a reason for visiting, and there was no point to pissing on the situation before they had learned that reason. He shook her hand as Sandra crossed her arms over her chest.

Cecily kept her eyes locked on Sandra. "My apologies if I've intruded, but I need to speak with you about an urgent matter."

"Come in," Max said. "Have a seat."

She glanced at the couch, and her pointed nose wriggled at an offensive odor. "I won't be long. I think I'll stand."

Sandra's jaw tightened. Max hurried between them. "Okay," he said. "Why don't you tell us what Tucker wants and you can be on your way."

Cecily chuckled — an off-putting, airy sound like a dog's squeaky toy that could barely squeak. "I'm not here on Tucker's behalf. Not in the least. I'm here for me and for me alone."

"Then why don't you tell us what it is you want."

"Your help, of course. You are one of the few people in this town, possibly in this entire world, that can actually help me because you are one of the few that has managed to face the Hull family and survive."

Max gestured to the trailer. "We do survive, but not unscathed."

Cecily chuckled again. Sandra's eyes narrowed, and Max wondered if the old cartoon image of steam boiling out of one's ears could actually happen.

Clearing his throat, he hoped the sound might snap Sandra into a more professional state-of-mind. To Cecily, he said, "Exactly how are you related to the Hulls?"

Her eyes perked up. "Ah, you're finally asking an intelligent question. That's good. I was beginning to think the family had overestimated you. Let me save you the trouble of taxing your brain too greatly. I'm the daughter of Terrance Hull. I'm the reason for all of this mess with Tucker." She raised a hand to stop Max's questions. "You see, the Hull family is a patriarchy. Except that's too simplistic. It's an extreme, orthodox patriarchy. Everything revolves around control of power through the male line."

"And you're the only child of Terrance Hull?"

"You *are* smart. Yes. Father had no other children. Only me. A daughter. He tried for more but Mother suffered complications — her uterus was not healthy enough, I suppose. After me, she couldn't have another child. Divorce was never an option. We are too religious a family to allow such a blemish. Father asked our witch to cast a spell that would help him gain an heir, but no spell could help Mother. And unfortunately for Father, other than a weak uterus, Mother's health was excellent. She will probably outlive him, and so, he could not hope to remarry and try with a younger woman."

"Couldn't he just get rid of her? Accidents happen in your family."

"My, my. I had heard that you thought low of us, but I had no idea how low. No, Mr. Porter, we do not murder our own to make life easier." Over her shoulder, she said to Sandra, "You better watch out for this one. If he doesn't like what you're doing, you might find yourself the victim of an accident."

Max grabbed Sandra's hand and yanked her close. Her fingers dug into his flesh. Better that than having to pry those fingers off of Cecily Hull's neck. "So, Terrance had you, and to your twisted family, that's a bad thing."

Ignoring the jab, Cecily continued. "It was Father's idea to bring back Tucker. Then, at least, the family could live under the sure hand of Tucker while waiting for me to produce a boy. That was their plan, anyway."

"You don't sound too keen on the whole idea."

"This is the twenty-first century. I grew up in a family stuck in the nineteenth — at least when it comes to views about women. So, no, I am not keen on the idea. In fact, I want to help my family modernize its views. I want to force the family to accept me as the new head. To do so requires the aid of special people with special skills. You and your little research firm are some of those people."

Max kept expecting a camera crew to pop through the door and inform him that he had been the target of some prank show. "You want to hire us to help you become the next head of the Hull family?"

"I want to hire you to do something you badly need done — get rid of Tucker Hull."

"I thought you didn't murder your own."

"Tucker's already dead. He's also unnatural and in my way."

"So, exceptions can be made."

"Always. In return for your assistance, you will receive substantial income, and I can easily throw in a better home. Most importantly, once Tucker Hull is no longer a problem, all of your unfortunate circumstances will go away. He is the reason you suffer. But when I lead the family, I will do away with such petty behavior. You'll be free to live, work, and prosper anywhere you desire. Nobody will be out to ruin you."

"Only if we help you, though. I mean, if you managed to take over the family without us, then this petty behavior against us will continue, right?"

"I suppose if you want to stay out of this and simply pray that I succeed, that I won't hold a grudge against you, and that I'll be benevolent toward your situation, you are free to do so. But only with your help will you ensure that I succeed, that I won't hold a grudge against you, and that I'll be benevolent toward your situation."

Sandra bumped Max aside. "That's it. Get out. I don't care if you're a Hull, I will not allow you to stand in my home and threaten us."

"I was not threatening you."

"Sure sounded like it to me."

"I assure you —"

"That's not worth much, is it? You got any references?"

"Excuse me?"

"References — people who can vouch for you."

Cecily stiffened her back. "I'm a Hull."

"That's the problem."

"I merely meant that —"

"We know exactly what you meant. You Hulls are nothing but a cancer to our life and we won't have anything to do with you. Go. Play your little family politics with someone else. We are not your pawns anymore."

Cecily held still and gazed down at Sandra. Max worried he would have to jump in to stop Sandra from throwing a punch, but then Cecily's lips broke into a snobbish grin. "My, my. You certainly do have spunk. What a shame you won't work with me." She leaned over. "You may want to rethink your position, but whatever you choose, I promise you I will become the next leader of the Hulls. So if you refuse to help me, you'd best stay out of my way."

With a calm gait, Cecily walked out of the trailer. She got into her car, a classic Porshe 911, and she drove away. As the sound of her engine receded, Sandra kicked a new dent into the wall.

"Damn, I wish I could have strangled that woman," she said. "The nerve of her coming here like she was doing us a favor by trying to force us back into that maze of crap they call a family. Can you believe that?"

Max had been married long enough to know Sandra well — good and bad. He knew she needed to vent off this anger, especially after their own fight, and he knew the best way to help her was to simply agree with her, to let her spout whatever she needed to say, and then later they could talk about this with rational thought. But he made a crucial mistake — he hesitated. Sandra turned toward him, her face a mixture of anger and confusion.

"Are you really thinking about taking her up on this?"

"Of course not." Max shook his head, but he couldn't stop his mouth. "But she does make a few good points."

"Good points? Are you crazy?"

"I only mean that without Tucker Hull our lives would be easier. Maybe it wouldn't be a bad idea to take a chance on her. Worst thing that happens is she turns out to be like all the other Hulls."

"Really? That's what you think is the worst? How about this — Tucker Hull slams Cecily into the ground and maintains control of the family. He's really pissed now and who can he look at to blame for this happening? Oh, I don't know, maybe those Porters who've screwed things up for him on several occasions. You think it's bad now, what happens when Tucker Hull really wants to hurt us? We'd be lucky if he only sends a hitman to murder us. More likely, we'll end up cursed, living out an eternity in some form of torture."

"If Hull wanted to curse us, he would have already. We're just not that important to him."

Max reached out but she slapped away his arms. "Well, dear Husband, let me ask you a question. Is gaining money and some false sense of security really worth selling your soul to the Hulls?"

"Honey, that's going a bit far. Maybe you're not seeing this clearly because it involves the Hulls."

"I'm prejudiced, now? Is that it?"

"That's not what I said."

Sandra stomped down the small aisle leading to the

Chapter 4

THE NEXT MORNING, Max said little to Sandra as she thumped a bowl on the counter, slammed cereal in the bowl, splashed on some milk, and clanged out a spoonful. She held the spoon at her mouth, a thought crossing her brow, and seemed about to speak. Instead, she clamped her mouth around the cereal and shoveled the rest in as fast as she could manage. With more clatter, she tossed the dirty bowl and spoon in the sink before going back into the bedroom. Shortly after, she emerged wearing her bakery clothes, grabbed a treat from the cookie jar, and left for work.

"Wow," Drummond said. "I've seen her give you the cold shoulder before but that was an arctic blast."

"It's worse than that." Max walked to the sink and cleaned out the dirty cereal bowl. "She doesn't have to work until this evening."

"Days like this one make me glad I never got married. At least, if she's got to work tonight, it'll make it easier for you to go the fights."

"I didn't say I was going."

"But the fix is for tonight. You can't turn down that kind of a sure thing. Come on. You need the money."

Heading toward the door, Max said, "I'll think about it."

"Great. So where are we going?"

"I'm going to the library."

Drummond's posture drooped. "The library? Why?"

"You said I should work on the case. Well, that's what I'm going to do. Sebastian Freeman hired me to find his family roots. I might as well start with that."

"I suppose that's a good idea." Drummond crossed his arms

as he floated alone in the living area. "Meet you back here tonight, okay?"

Max held back a laugh. "You aren't coming with me?"

"Come on. I don't do the bookworm stuff."

"See you tonight, then."

As Max drove toward Wake Forest University, he felt pleased with Drummond's predictability. If ever he needed to be alone, the library was to one place he knew he could count on. Drummond hated that kind of research. Too quiet, Max guessed.

The Z. Smith Reynolds Library continued to be his favorite in the area. For him, university libraries had always touched on an extra level of importance to the research he had to do. He knew it was a silly idea, but he couldn't deny it, either. Seeing students hunched over books made up part of it. Also, the types of academic materials found at the University's library mattered, too. It was purely an aesthetic, though. Max knew that. Still, he loved that library. Stepping inside, inhaling that unique aroma of old paper and listening to that muted hush which enveloped all libraries, Max's body settled into it all like coming home after a long day of travel.

"Mr. Porter, you're back," Leon Moore said as Max walked by the main desk.

Leon was a tall, hefty black man who had worked in the library for the past year. He had a thick beard that created some definition to his round, balding head. A few days back, when Max had asked for some help, Leon took great interest in the work and went far above the call of a librarian's duty to aid him. Then again, part of the reason Max preferred researching in the library over the Internet was that every librarian he had ever encountered went far above the call of duty.

Max waved hello, and as he set up at a nearby table — one under the open skylights — Leon shuffled over. The man walked with a limp, and he had a slight bend to his back, both of which made him appear far older than the truth — forty-three.

"I was wondering if I'd see you again," Leon said.

"Why wouldn't you?"

"I saw on the news this morning all about Sebastian Freeman. Somebody killed him. I figured you wouldn't be researching for him anymore since he isn't around anymore. Unless that was some other Sebastian Freeman."

"Unfortunately, it was him. But I'm still working on the research. I don't like to let stuff like that go unfinished. Besides, he's got family. They might appreciate knowing where they came from as much as he wanted to know."

Clapping his hands together — a near-perfect imitation of Drummond — Leon opened one of Max's notebooks. "Where are we today?"

"Well, we know that after the Emancipation Proclamation and moreso after the Civil War, a lot of former slaves took on the name Freeman. But following the standard records searches, we got two strong possibilities for Sebastian's great-great-great grandfather, both of which were plantation slaves in Virginia. The real problem, the one I think he was most interested in, was his mother's side."

In general, plantation records kept in the nineteenth century were only as thorough as the record keeper wanted them to be. Some families were meticulous. Some were spotty. Some could not have cared less. There were no computers, no deep data mines, and no need for such things. Add to that the fact that most general records — such as marriages and real estate — only concerned males, and the problem of tracing a mother's line back through slavery became a massive fishing expedition armed with a hook and no bait.

In the case of Sebastian Freeman, Max only had the first name of his great-great grandmother — Lilla. The name didn't show up anywhere useful which both disappointed Max and gave him hope. The disappointment came from failure. The hope came from knowing that when he did find the name, it was unusual enough that the odds were much higher that it belonged to Freeman's relative.

Several hours in, Max had found little that he could work with. Leon came up with a book of photos taken during the

Reconstruction, but without Sebastian to look through them, Max merely saw a sea of faces. As dinner approached, he decided to call it a day.

Normally, he would go home and enjoy dinner with Sandra, but that wouldn't be happening until they got through their fight. Instead, Max drove to the downtown section of the city and walked along the numerous restaurants. He knew many of them to be excellent places to eat, but he couldn't afford them anymore. With five dollars in his pocket, he decided he could manage half-a-sub at Subway, and as he bit into his meager meal, Drummond appeared across from him.

"You ready for tonight?" he asked.

To hide that Max spoke to an empty chair, he wiped his mouth with a paper napkin. "I'm still not convinced this is a good idea."

"Nonsense. You know I'm right. I usually am, and this time, I definitely am. The facts are simple. You need money. Stop acting like a fool and be a man."

"Really? You're going to try to shame me into submission with a 'be a man' taunt?"

"Listen, if I could make the bet for you, I would. But I have this unfortunate condition of being dead. So, let's get going."

Max glanced at his watch. "The fight isn't for hours."

"You can't just show up. Are you crazy? We need to check out the place first. Make sure the only thing underhanded going on is the fixed fight. Plus, they often have up-and-comer fights earlier on, so you can go in and appear more natural by watching a few fights before making your bet."

"I don't even have any cash."

"All the more reason to get started now. We go to the bank and get a hundred for the bet."

Max tried not to choke, but some teen girls threw him an odd look and some giggles. Without another word, he forced down the rest of his meal, tossed the trash, and hurried to his car. At least he could talk freely in there — most people would assume he was on Bluetooth or singing with the radio.

"No way can I bet a hundred dollars. I only ever got two

hundred from Freeman, and that's got to help pay bills. Not to mention that Sandra's already pissed off. She finds out about this, she'll kill me."

"Not with 10-to-1 odds. You'll bring back a thousand dollars. What's wrong with that?"

Max wanted to argue more, but he noticed that the car headed toward the bank. Part of him had already decided and there seemed little point in fighting it further.

Chapter 5

By the time Max turned off Old US 52 into the parking lot of a vacant building, his mind had become a mush of conflicting thoughts. Looking at the people getting out of their cars or dismounting their motorcycles, Max knew he didn't belong. In Winston-Salem, the Southeastern section of the city was predominately Hispanic — most of the signs were in Spanish and much of the conversation Max heard had the flow of Spanish. His aptitude for languages had never gone beyond failing Spanish 2 in high school, so he couldn't be sure.

Not only was Max out of place, but his intentions were the kind that could get him in a lot of trouble. This was a dangerous place and betting on a fixed fight seemed like a dumb move — like robbing the people running this operation. But Drummond's words hit the bull's-eye over and over — they needed the money.

Stepping out of his beat up Honda, the cold air chilled his nose and ears. Not as cold as the silence from Sandra, though — she hadn't even bothered to call wondering where he was. And beyond her, he had the name Hull floating in his brain.

No. He had to put all those thoughts aside. He had come here for a simple purpose. He should focus on that, get the job done, and leave as fast as possible.

He headed toward the entrance. The building had been a small warehouse or machine shop before. A loading dock large enough for two trucks ran along the front. Off-white paint peeled on all the walls and the rest of the building had a utilitarian, boxy look.

Three elderly Hispanic men walked in, one using a cane, and that sight eased Max's nerves. How dangerous could the place actually be, if those men entered without fear? It also pleased him that he would not be the oldest man in the building.

As he entered, a table blocked the door leading to the main room — a fight was already in progress and the crowd's cheers rumbled out to the line of men waiting to get in. Two guys large enough to be nightclub bouncers stood at the table. One collected a twenty dollar entrance fee while the second offered a betting form similar to what one saw at a horse race.

Max paid, took his form, and noticed that the layout of names followed the list he had swiped from Baxter House. He walked into the main room. The noise assaulted his ears as did the thick odor of sweat. This place had been designed to store boxes for shipping, not run a sporting event. Max wondered if this little business operated under the property owner's nose or if the owner got a cut of the proceeds.

Drummond clapped his hands as he slid alongside Max. "I'm so glad you decided to come here. I haven't been to a local fight in years. Decades, really. I'm looking forward to this."

Max found an empty spot along the temporary metal bleachers set up around the ring. The ring itself looked professional enough. Two racks of lights had been mounted on thick poles, and long cables ran off to a generator. A few space heaters warmed those working the judges table and elsewhere, but mostly it was the body heat of the crowd that kept the temperature up. Still, everyone kept their winter coats on, and hot coffee appeared to sell far better than cold beer.

Two sweating middleweights slugged it out while the ref circled the fight. They kept clutching each other and some in the crowd booed. Neither fighter moved with much gusto. Max figured he had come near the end of this particular bout.

"What are you sitting down for?" Drummond asked. "Go make your bet."

"Relax. That fight isn't for a while and I want to look around first." Now that he was there, Max started to wonder about Sebastian, the murder, Baxter House, and the paper that had led him to the Midnight Fights. How did those things connect? And who actually owned that house?

That question smacked Max in the head as hard as the punches being thrown in the ring. He had been so wrapped up in losing his client, his fight with Sandra, and his visit from Cecily Hull, that he never asked some of the most basic questions. It wasn't Sebastian's house — the man had made it quite clear how little money he had. It didn't look lived in, though it was immaculate and clean. Yet books overflowed the shelves of that study and those papers were on the desk. Somebody used that space. Why had the police bothered calling in Max when they had more obvious people to inquire about — like the owner of that house?

"Max, wake up," Drummond said, snapping his fingers before Max's face. "You'll miss an entire fight at this rate. Now, get down there and make your bet."

"Maybe it'll be better to watch this time."

With a sigh that sounded more like a haunted moan, Drummond said, "I understand you're nervous, but you're going to win. So, relax. Besides, nobody comes here just to watch. If you don't bet, people are going to get suspicious, and you've already got enough unwanted attention being here. You don't exactly fit in."

"I noticed."

"Then get moving."

Grumbling that he didn't even understand this sport, Max walked over to a crowded table where men shouted out names and numbers. He nudged his way into the line and when he reached one of the house bookies, the man at the table spit out words rapid fire. It took Max a second to realize the man spoke in Spanish.

"I want to make a bet," Max said.

The man smiled and shook his head. "No problem, man. Who you want and how much?"

Max glanced at the betting form, but he already knew the names on the list. "Gonzalez for two hundred." He half-expected the bookie to throw out a *Jeopardy*-like answer waiting for the winning question.

"What round?"

"Huh?"

As if talking to an idiot, and Max couldn't blame him for that, the man said, "You can bet on the round Gonzalez wins or you can bet on a TKO or on a decision at the end."

"Can't I just pick the winner?"

"Yeah," the man said with a bit of disappointment.

When Max got back to his seat, he told Drummond what had happened. Drummond nodded. "Place like this, the payout doubles if you pick the winning round, but if you're wrong, you lose the whole thing. Since the fight is fixed, they already know you're gonna win, so by not picking the round, you guaranteed they'll be losing some money to you tonight."

"You couldn't have told me that before I went to make the bet?"

"I thought you knew this kind of thing."

"What kind of thing? I've never been to a boxing match before." Two men further along the bench glanced at Max before shifted away from him. In a lower voice, he added, "All I know is that two guys get in the ring and beat each other to a pulp."

"It's a lot more than that."

A portly man in a tuxedo stepped into the ring. "Gentleman," he bellowed, and for the first time, Max noticed that the audience was entirely male. As the man spoke, the first fighter entered wearing a white robe. Two men — his trainer and another — entered with him. "For the next bout, in the right corner, weighing in at 187 pounds with a record of five knockouts, ten wins, and two losses, Hershel Jackson."

The audience cheered and Jackson walked around the ring with his gloved hands held high. He was a muscular black man with a vicious look in his eyes. Max wondered how much they had to pay the guy to take this dive because he certainly looked like he could win a fight with ease.

"And in the left corner," the announcer continued as the other fighter approached, "weighing in at 183 pounds with a record of one knockout, four wins, and four losses, Hector

Gonzalez."

Gonzalez bounded into the ring, his handlers ripping off the gold and silver robe, and he pranced around the ring thumping his chest. Some cheered, but the majority booed. Max hoped the upset that was about to happen didn't cause a riot.

Moments later, the ring cleared, the ref spoke to the fighters, the bell rang, and the fight began. The two men circled each other, jabbing out their arms, but not making any big moves.

"This is it?" Max said. "I thought they were supposed to be pummeling each other."

"You sure got blood-thirsty fast." Drummond stared at Max a moment and finally gestured to the ring. "Look, this isn't some barbaric gladiator kind of thing. Yeah, it's a fight, but it's really like a living chess match. Lots of strategy and thought goes into every moment. See, right now, there's plenty going on. They're feeling each other out — trying to determine each other's fighting style. Also, they're quickly learning their distances — how close can they get without getting hurt. Now, did you see that? Jackson shifted his feet and started circling the other direction."

"So?"

"Well, Gonzalez did the same. So, Jackson just took control of their movement. That's important. Whoever controls the ring usually controls the fight. Now, all those little jabs are for more than just distance. Each fighter is trying to force a reaction from the other. If I keep jabbing at you, and I notice that every time you flinch back to right, then when I'm ready, I fake a jab, you flinch right, and my full power punch is waiting for you in that spot I know you're going for. Get it?"

"They're trying to set up a real strong punch."

"Exactly. There's emotional stuff going on too — intimidation, breaking confidence, things like that."

Though Max did not catch all of what Drummond had said, he understood enough to see that more went on in the fight than he had realized. He even experienced a little tremble in his chest when he caught that Gonzalez tried to change the direction of the circling but Jackson turned that shift into an assault. The fighters exchanged four hard punches before clenching up. Without Drummond's explanation, Max saw that while clenched, Jackson threw two more punches to the ribs. They weren't just hugging each other, buying time — they were inflicting body blows in each clench that would add up over the course of the fight and become crucial later on.

Except this fight is fixed, Max thought. None of it mattered. It was no more real than a reality show on television.

"Wow," Drummond said. "Jackson's putting on a heck of a show. He's a real fighter. It's got to be burning him bad to take this dive."

As the fight continued into round after round, Max lost interest. No real point when he knew that no matter how bad Gonzalez looked to be doing, he would soon be making a miraculous comeback. Instead, Max scanned the crowd. He wondered what would happen if all those hard-working men learned that if they had bet on Jackson, they had no way of winning. In such a small place, the outcome would be fatal to a lot of innocent people.

Max froze as his eyes rested on one man in particular — a black man with a stark white horseshoe of hair running around his head. Looking closer, Max saw the same overweight body, the same hooked nose, and — when the man cheered for Jackson — the same discolored yellow tooth.

"Why would he be here?"

Drummond kept his attention on the fight. "What? Who?"

"There's a guy down there — I swear he was one of the crime scene techs at Baxter House."

"You think that's odd? Be glad that's the worst thing he's doing. Cops and techs and all the so-called 'good guys' have as many vices as the rest of us. Maybe even more since they're surrounded by it all day long."

"Yeah, but that seems like too much of a coincidence, and you've certainly made it clear that there are no coincidences."

Drummond finally turned his head to look at the man. "You're certain it's the same guy?"

"I think so." Max dug out his phone. He figured he'd try to

take a picture of the man, maybe zoom in, and see if a closer look helped.

"No need for that. You're right. It's him."

"How do you know? You weren't there yet when I bumped into him."

"I know because I just saw him glance up here, and now he's leaving."

Drummond was right. The large man had sidestepped his way off the bleacher and walked around back.

"Come on," Max said. "Something's up."

"You check it out. I want to see the rest of this fight."

"You know how it's going to end."

"A well-choreographed fix can be every bit as entertaining as a fair fight."

With a disgruntled huff, Max climbed over the two benches in front of him, walked behind the bleachers, and moved at a brisk pace in the direction of the man. He couldn't run — too many people crowding the area plus doing so would have drawn too much attention. The heavy coffee aroma did little to mask the foul odors of all these bodies. Max didn't want to know why his shoes kept sticking to the floor.

He turned the corner in time to see the man open a door and walk through. Maybe he hadn't seen Max in the bleachers. Maybe he simply needed to use a restroom. But with the building technically vacant, the place had no running water — no restrooms would be working. The men were expected to pee outside. Anything else was expected to wait until they went somewhere else.

The crowd broke out a surprised gasp. Looked like Gonzalez had finally started his comeback. Max opened the door and peered in — a long hall lit by several battery-operated lanterns. No sign of the big man.

At the far end, one door stood ajar and dim light cut into the hall. Max could hear murmured voices. He wanted to call Drummond over, but it would take too much time to get back to his seat, grab the ghost, and return. He certainly couldn't yell for Drummond.

Ignoring the itch on the back of his neck — the one digging under his skin, crawling up to his brain and shouting *Don't be stupid!* — Max entered the hall. The sharp thuds of the landed blows and the deep grunts of the wounded fighters echoed down the hall turning it into a carnival funhouse trick. Max's pulse quickened and his mouth dried.

He tried the first doors on either side. Both were locked. Laughter from down the hall. Deep-toned laughter — the kind that belonged to big, dangerous men. He thought he could hear guns being loaded. But he shook off the thought — only his imagination. For all he knew, the sound belonged to the click of beer cans against a metal table.

He tried another door. Locked. He needed some place he could hide while attempting to eavesdrop. The big man had been at Baxter House, *and* he had looked up at Max during the fight, choosing that moment to leave. Maybe he could convince himself that one of these had been coincidence. But all of it? Not likely. Not remotely likely.

About halfway down the hall, Max tried another door, and this time the knob turned. Licking the sweat off his lip, he eased the door open. But as he pushed it quietly in, someone took hold and yanked it from his hand.

Max took one look in the room and his stomach flipped. In the center of the room sat an elderly woman. She had long, curly gray hair and deeply wrinkled skin. Her eyes were clouded over. She wore numerous scarves, shreds of dresses, and bruises where clothes didn't cover her arms or legs. She looked like a storybook gypsy that had been dragged behind a pickup truck for a few miles.

Her chair had been set in the middle of a large painted circle. Numerous symbols adorned the circle. Seven candles lined the outside of the circle and provided the only light in the room. Though Max didn't know the specific symbols, he had seen enough spells and curses to know he had stumbled into something no good. This woman was a witch casting a spell.

She raised her hand at Max, and her palm bled from where she had dug another symbol into her skin — a swirling sign similar to a yin-yang but with a river-like path running through the middle. Her dead eyes stared at him, and her mouth moved without sound. Then she screamed.

"Here! Here!" she said.

From down the hall, Max heard voices. "Is that her? You hear that?"

"Crap," Max said as he darted out of the room.

"Oooo!" The witch's voice swirled around Max as he rushed down the hall. Nearing the main room where sounds of the fight rushed back at him, the doors opened and two burly men stepped in.

One lifted a cell phone to his mouth. There was a high-pitched beep. "Yeah, we got him."

Max whirled around and tore off in the other direction. He sped by the witch's door and heard her crying out. The men behind him approached with caution. Max figured they knew he had no way out and they didn't want to get hurt if he panicked. *Too late for that,* he thought as his heart raced fast enough to win a Nascar event.

He tried a door on his left. Locked. He glanced back. The two men blocked the hall with their bulk. He shuffled down to the next door, this one on the right. It opened!

Dashing in, he saw another door on the opposite side of the room. He hurried across, stumbling into a chair, and tried the handle. It opened into another hall.

Max sprinted off to the left, randomly trying doors, hoping to lose the men in this maze. But the more turns he made, the more doors he went through, the more lost he became. When he cut across another room, he entered a hall that looked familiar. They all looked similar, though.

Sweat poured down his sides and his ragged breathing rang in his ears. He had to think. But he could hear the men approaching. He dashed on, turned a corner, and all hope sank. The hallway became a tunnel with only one light sitting halfway down and one door at the end. A sign hung above the door with the word EXIT above. This would have been a welcome sight, if not for the two-hundred pounds of muscle standing in front of the door.

If Max had to be beaten, he figured one beating would be better than two. He walked toward the exit and tried to ignore the footsteps behind him. The huge man blocking the exit crossed his arms but remained in his spot.

One of the men behind Max said, "Hey, man, c'mon. You got nowhere to go."

Max continued walking.

"Just come with us. Don't make us hurt you."

Max pressed on. He knew he should stop. He knew that they had him no matter what he did and that wherever they took him, more pain would follow, so why make the pain start now? But he couldn't stop his legs even if he tried.

The boulder in front of him appeared to grow larger. He became a mountain blocking Max's way. The mountain put out its hand, much like the witch had done, only this hand had no bloody symbol carved in the palm — this hand merely said *Stop, or you'll be sorry.*

Max cringed as he stepped closer. But the man's hand started to shiver. His eyes widened and his mouth dropped. The two behind Max stopped, and one of them muttered, "What's wrong?"

The mountain dropped to his knees. Drummond floated behind with his hand buried into the guard's back. The ghost screamed out as the guard did so, too.

Hearing Drummond's pain snapped Max into action. He bolted ahead, leaped over the guard, and slammed through the exit. The two behind him followed, one stopping to help the injured guard.

"Get to your car," Drummond said, slouching in the hallway. "I'll catch up in a minute."

Max darted across the parking lot, heading straight for his Honda. The frozen night air cut into his lungs, but he kept running. His mind could only process one thought — get to the car. So, even as he noticed the wide puddle on the broken asphalt, his mind never warned him that in North Carolina the night air often dropped low enough to freeze water. He hit the ice and his legs went out from under him. His side slammed on the hard ground and he rolled a few feet further.

As he struggled to get back up, a meaty hand grabbed his shoulder. He looked up in time to see a tight fist approaching his face.

Chapter 6

MAX'S EYES FLUTTERED OPEN against harsh fluorescent lights. Cold concrete pressed against his back while he smelled old feet from the thin pillow under his head. That poor head — the ache started in the back near his neck, wrapped straight over, and settled on the bruises covering the right side of his face. When his eyes finally adjusted, Max confirmed where he thought he was — jail.

Groaning, he sat up. The cot offered nothing in the way of comfort, but he hadn't expected much either. Off to his left, through the jail cell's bars, he saw the tan wall of a hallway.

"So, this is jail," he muttered. He had never been in a cell before. His calm demeanor surprised him at first. But the more he thought about it, he realized that he remained calm partly because his body hurt too much to worry and partly because he knew he wouldn't stay in that cell for long. He couldn't imagine the charges being anything worse than attending an illegal boxing event or disorderly conduct. Whatever the charges, his record didn't have anything serious before. He might end up with some community service hours, but it wasn't as if he stared at years behind bars. A few hours, a day at most — he could handle that.

"Well, ain't this a pickle?" Drummond said as he entered through the concrete wall opposite Max.

Max thought he should revise how long he could endure being in a cell, if Drummond decided to stay. "No need to hang around. I'm sure I'll be out soon."

"You could use a few more hours in here. Your face looks horrible."

"Gee, thanks."

"They worked you over hard."

"I had no idea. I thought the pain in my head came from you yapping away all the time."

"Hey, don't get all uppity with me. I saved your ass, remember."

Max scooted to the edge of the cot, leaned over, and cupped his chin. "I know. Thank you. Seriously. Anyway, what did you find out?"

"Huh?"

"Come on. I can see the sunlight down the hall. I know you didn't spend the whole evening watching over me. Not with all that happened. So, what did you get?"

Drummond grinned as he tipped his hat back. "Good to see you're really getting the hang of all this. Well, while you slept off that beating, I followed that fat man to his home."

"Do you have to say it like that?"

"Like what?"

"Like being fat is a bad thing." Max waved off his complaint when he saw the confusion in Drummond's face. "Forget it."

"You people today get so crazy about the names of things. Sheesh."

"Right. We're all PC screwed up. Now, get on with it — you followed the *heavyset* man, the crime scene tech, to his home."

Drummond peeked down into his coat pocket, listened, and shrugged. "Okay, okay. Leed wants you to know that really it was his idea to follow the guy home."

"I don't care who had the idea. It was Leed's idea. Fine. And?"

"And his name is Luther Boer. He lives on the eastern edge of the city line in a crappy apartment. Married. Didn't get a good look at the wife. She slept under a ton of covers, trying to save money on heating. No kids. That's about it for now."

Max rubbed his temples to stave off the pounding in his head from getting worse. "Thanks. At least that gives us a little something to go on."

"*Little?* You got thumped in the head too much if that's what you think."

"Maybe I did. What am I missing?"

With an impatient huff, Drummond said, "Add it all up. You're called to a murder scene in which Luther Boer is one of the crime scene techs. It just so happens that on the desk of the room in which the murder occurred, there are papers with information on a fixed fight. Luther is at that fight. Want to bet which fighter he laid money on? If those things aren't connected, I'll quit smoking."

"You quit smoking the moment you died."

"Then I'll figure out how a ghost can smoke, I'll start smoking, and then quit again. Point is this — if Luther didn't kill Sebastian directly for those fight fixes, he certainly was involved. In fact, it looks like Sebastian was in on running this fight scam."

"Damn." Max clamped his mouth shut, holding back the urge to vomit. "Why do the weird ones always find me?"

"Nothing weird about a fixed fight. They happen all the time."

"You didn't see why everybody tried to beat me up."

"They didn't try, they succeeded."

Max touched his swollen cheek. "Yeah, well, the reason was that I stumbled upon a witch casting a spell. I don't know what she was doing exactly, but I'm guessing it had to do with the fight."

"That explains what happened after you left. I told you at the fight it looked like Jackson wanted to win. When Gonzalez made his comeback, I thought I was seeing a master actor in Jackson. The expression on his face — he couldn't believe Gonzalez suddenly fought back. I've seen fighters take dives before. They don't look like that."

"So, Jackson didn't take a dive. The people running the fight used a witch to give Gonzalez an edge."

"More like a sledgehammer, but yup. That's what happened."

"Maybe Sebastian was in on this scam. Luther figured it out. Then what? He kills Sebastian?"

"Probably tried blackmail first. They met at Baxter House

because it's vacant. Sebastian refuses to yield to Luther's demands, Luther loses his temper, takes a swing at Sebastian, they struggle, and he accidentally kills your client."

It fit together, but Max got the feeling they were pounding those puzzle pieces into place. Something was off. Lack of blood, for one thing. A struggle and accidental murder would have left a wound on the body and blood on the floor — but none had been found at the scene.

"Talking to yourself?" Detective Rolson said as he blustered down the hall toward Max's cell. "You know, that's the first sign of insanity from incarceration."

Max waited as the heavy steps of the man approached. When Rolson finally appeared at the door, he leaned his shoulder on the frame and grinned. His blond hair seemed brighter this time as did his entire demeanor.

"I'd like a lawyer," Max said.

Drummond said, "That's right. Never talk to these guys without a lawyer."

Rolson raised his hands with a fake, staccato laugh. "Easy there. No need for lawyers. You're not getting charged with anything. In fact, you've been processed. I'm here to let you out."

"Since when do detectives handle this kind of thing?"

"Oh, not usually, I admit. But I wanted to have a little chat with you before you go." Max edged back in the cell, and Rolson made that same horrible laughing sound. "Now, now, no need to worry. I wasn't implying anything but a real chat. I'm not going to hurt you."

Drummond shifted closer to Rolson. "You want me to freeze his brain? I'll do it gladly." Max shot Drummond a harsh look. "I was joking. Sheesh. If you want to be like that, then I'll go wait for you outside." With that, Drummond left.

Rolson pressed up against the bars, his belly pushing through, and snorted hard as if he might spit into the cell. "I'm a little troubled by what I see. I got a guy whose name comes up in a murder investigation, and only a couple days later, same guy gets hauled in for disorderly conduct at an underground, illegal boxing match. Quite a coincidence. Now, something I've learned over my years as a detective is that there are no coincidences. So, you being at these places — this troubles me."

"Me, too."

"Don't be a wiseass. I'm trying to help you here."

Rolson unlocked the door and slid it open. Even when opening, it made the telltale clanking sound of finality. Max wondered if the companies that made these doors had purposely designed them to make that sound.

Rolson stood firm in his position, forcing Max to sidestep in order to exit the cell. As he passed through, Rolson poked him in the chest several times. "You listen to me. Whatever you're involved in, get out now. You're clearly much too frail to run around with people who can make your face look as bad as it does — people who commit murder. You're not ready for these kinds of people. You don't know what you're up against, and from what I've seen in this world, you don't want to know."

"Thanks for the advice. I'll consider it."

"No, you won't. I've seen enough like you in my time. I know how this plays out." Rolson hefted his pants up and readjusted his shirt. "Well, the advice I've given you, that's the carrot. Here's the stick — you got connected to my murder case, you got busted at this fight, that's your two strikes, as far as I'm concerned. You so much as get a speeding ticket, I'm going to find out about it, and I'll drag your ass in. You understand me?"

Max's muscles tensed. Part of him wanted to deck Rolson and send him sprawling to the ground. In his younger days, Max might have done just that, but he clenched his teeth and in a low growl said, "Yes, sir, Detective Rolson. I understand you one hundred percent, five-by-five, and crystal clear."

Not content to let Max have the last word, Rolson gave Max's shoulder a little shove down the hall. "We'll see. Perhaps your wife can keep you in line."

Max looked back. "My wife?"

"Yeah. She's the one that came to get you."

Max swallowed against the lump growing in his throat. Of course, Sandra would be the one to pick him up. He shouldn't have expected otherwise — the only other living person he knew well in this city was Leon at the library. But knowing that Sandra waited for him, knowing how bad things were between them, knowing that he had no other option — he feared this might be the trial that broke their marriage.

As he walked to the end of the holding area and waited for Rolson to unlock the door into the rest of the police station, Max concentrated on keeping the tears from falling down his face. Despite the fights, despite the down times, despite every negative instance in their marriage, Max loved Sandra unquestionably. The mere taste of a possible divorce nauseated him, and his heart cracked under the possibility that he had gone too far.

She stood at a tall counter, filling out some forms, and Max had a moment in which he watched her without her knowing. *So beautiful.* A simple enough thought, but one that kept repeating in his head, and in its repetition, the words took on deeper layers. Her beauty went far beyond her physical attributes, and his love followed her into her depths.

When she tilted her head towards him, her eyes glistened over. She rushed into his arms. "Are you okay?" She looked as his bruised face, putting out her fingers to touch his skin but holding back for fear of hurting him.

"I'm fine," he said. "Thanks for getting me out."

Satisfied that he had not been harmed, she slapped his arm. "What the hell were you thinking?"

Max heard a snicker from behind. No need to look. He knew the sound of Drummond all too well. Besides, he didn't want to look over and see Rolson's smugness staring back at him.

They all stayed quiet until they were in the car and on the road home. Only then did Sandra speak, and Max shuddered at the worry in her voice. "Let's start with the obvious. How much trouble are we in?"

"I don't know. I'm not even sure what's going on."

"Drummond?" she said, glancing in the rearview mirror.

Drummond leaned forward. "He's telling you fair and square. You got yourself a dead body, a suspicious crime tech, fixed fights, and a witch. I couldn't tell you what that adds up to for certain."

"Okay, then," she said, running a yellow light as she headed out of the city. "With a witch involved, that means the Hulls. And if the Hulls are involved, that means Cecily Hull's visit was no accident."

Max leaned his forehead on the cold window. "I'm really sick of them. Part of me wants to help Cecily just to get rid of the rest of them."

Sandra poked the control console, trying to get the car's heating to kick in, but only a lukewarm trickle of air came out of the vents. "Let's focus on things that make sense."

"Nothing in this makes sense."

"Then let's look at it like a new case and go from there."

Drummond nodded. "You listen to her. She's still the smartest of you two."

"Okay," Max said. "I'll start fresh on this. Drummond and I will hit it all in the morning."

"Me, too," Sandra said.

"Nice of you to offer, but you'll be at work."

Sandra turned onto the gravel drive leading into the trailer park. "Oh, didn't I mention? I quit that job."

"Are you joking?"

She parked and faced him. "The Hulls are not going to leave us alone. You know that very well. Whatever's going on here, it involves them, and they've got to be dealt with. Working at the bakery won't help us do that, and if we don't deal with the Hulls, my part-time job won't matter. We'll be lucky if we make it to Christmas alive."

Drummond swished out of the car and put out his arms. "Looks like Max Porter Research and Investigations is back in action!"

Max cocked an eyebrow at his wife. "Since when is that our

name?"

"I think he just coined it. Kind of like it, though."

As Sandra exited the car, Max let his head loll back. He didn't deserve her. Knowing that his fears of ending their marriage had vanished only underscored how much he needed her. For a moment, his mind locked on one simple thought, *What an incredible woman.*

She knocked on the car door and gestured for him to get moving. As usual, she was right. They had a lot to do.

Chapter 7

MAX BOUNDED INTO THE LIBRARY, ready to tackle the research and find a solution. With Sandra's aid, he knew they could beat the Hulls — they had done so before — and he marveled at his own idiocy for having doubted her in the first place. He glanced at his wrist and considered having the words SHE'S ALWAYS ON YOUR SIDE tattooed to remind him that she was there for him when things got tough.

"You in a car accident?" Leon asked, his face wrinkling at the sight of Max's bruises.

"Looks worse than it is." Max smiled until his injured skin complained.

"Need any help today?"

"If you got the time, I'm always grateful for your help."

With that, Leon and Max went to work. As they navigated their way through online searches and poured over books found in dark corners of the library, Max found his brain falling easily into the rhythms of research. It helped knowing that at the same time, Drummond and Leed searched for Sebastian Freeman's ghost and Sandra dug up whatever information she could find on Luther Boer.

After a few hours of work, Max had formed a clear picture of North Carolina after the Civil War. It wasn't pretty. The North had devastated the South. Directly, Northern soldiers raided towns, killed civilians, and ravaged the lands. They behaved like conquerors — which in some ways, they were. Indirectly, the financial toll of running the war and losing much of their industry in the process struck the South hard. The emotional loss hit hardest of all. They needed to rebuild — both physically and mentally.

Problems started immediately. Carpetbaggers popped up before the canon smoke had cleared. These were Northerners or turncoats who now entered North Carolina politics and leveraged the black vote in order to gain office. Many whites saw these men as opportunists who used the black people in ways every bit as awful as slavery.

On the other end were the scalawags — disenfranchised rebels, many of whom fought for the South. What kind of life could they live now that the world they had built lay in ruin? The things they valued no longer were acceptable by the law, yet the land was filled with people who still wanted to fight the war.

It was a confusing, angry time. Every new law that came out of the North seemed designed to punish the Southerners — even as the North publicly said they wouldn't exact retribution.

"You know," Leon said, looking up from one dusty volume, "it's kind of interesting that when Lincoln was assassinated, many in the South cheered. They were thrilled to be rid of him. But I believe that if he had survived, a lot of the problems the South had to deal with wouldn't have happened. He seemed to understand that losing the war was punishment enough. He would have had a hard fight with Congress, but I think he might have kept the country on a better path."

Max often talked to his books while doing research. Having Leon around made him feel as if his books were talking back.

"Might never have been a KKK if Lincoln had survived," Max said.

Leon gave the idea some thought before shaking his head. "Maybe it wouldn't have become as big and powerful as it did, but too many white people hated black people. Too many more feared what we'd do after being treated so horribly for so long — especially if we got organized. After all, there were more blacks than whites at the time. So, I think the KKK or some group like it was inevitable."

Max had to agree. They both had uncovered enough newspaper articles depicting the latest lynching to know that fear and hatred flowed like the blood of soldiers on the battlefield. In fact, right after the Civil War had ended, maintaining order became the primary job of most leaders. Some attempted to use local law enforcement as well as political maneuvers. Others called on federal troops to force their way in.

Every night was fraught with violence. Every night ratcheted up the fear. Black people worried the Ku Klux Klan or some other white supremacy group would come after them. White people feared the black men would riot and tear apart the town.

It reached a point so bad that Congress enacted three laws, the last in 1871 known as the Enforcement Act which gave the President the power to suspend habeas corpus when combating the KKK and other groups like it.

Max shut one of the books with a hard thump. "How are we going to find one nearly nameless girl in the middle of this kind of chaos? People were bad enough at record-keeping to begin with, but with nightly raids and constant threats, too many of the black populace were on the move. Leaving for the North, running from the most dangerous towns, getting out as fast as they could. It's not as if these people were giving the post office a forwarding address."

Leon scratched the back of his head. "None of my business, so I won't be offended if you tell me to kiss off, but I got to ask — what's wrong? I mean, I've never seen you this worked up over researching."

"I'm sure you haven't."

"I got to be honest, seeing you all beat up and right after reading about Sebastian Freeman being murdered — should I be worried?"

"Nobody's coming after you. You've got nothing to tell them, anyway."

"But there is a *them?*"

"Yeah, there is. If you want to stop helping me, I understand. No reason for you to risk anything."

"You just said nobody would be coming for me. Now, I'm risking something? Which is it?"

Max paused long enough to give an answer serious thought.

Showing impressive patience, Leon waited, his expression never betraying any fear or concern. "I don't think you're in any real danger, but the people I'm dealing with are dangerous. They might approach you, might give you a hard time. They'll want to know what I've been researching and how far I got. Stuff like that."

"Look here, I'm a librarian, not whatever you are. I like history and family and spiritual, respectful, intelligent debate. I'm not a fighter, and I don't do illegal things."

"And I wouldn't ask you to."

"Okay, then. Long as that's clear, what do you want me to tell them?"

"The truth, of course — that you helped me search for Sebastian's family and we never could find anyone on his mother's side. You only know I wanted this info for Sebastian, that he was my client, and you found it strange that I continued to look into it even after Sebastian's death."

"But what if you find out more?"

"I think as far as you remember, nothing else happened. You can decide whether that's truth or lie by staying here or not. I won't force you to stay."

Leon chuckled to himself, smiling and giving a little shake but making no sound. He opened the book Max had closed and tapped the pages. "So, we're looking for Miss Lilla with no last name and we know she was alive during part of the Reconstruction because she marries the first Freeman that led to Sebastian."

"Right," Max said, holding back the urge to hug Leon. "We also know she lived long enough to have at least one child. So, if we assume she was a normal girl and married between fourteen and twenty, at the latest, that means she would have had to be born no later than 1851."

"Yup. And that means, if she lived a normal life, she would be dying around 1900 at the earliest. That'd give her about a good fifty years."

"I think it's a safe bet. If she had died young or outlived most, or if she had died from something unusual, we would know. Stories like that often made the papers, and they last a long time in a family. Especially a black family."

Leon pulled back. "What the heck's that supposed to mean?"

Max cocked his head to the side. "Really, Leon? You think I'm suddenly a racist?" Leon didn't back down. "Fine. The majority of black people in America descend from slaves. The majority of slaves were not permitted to learn reading and writing. Couple that with the oral African traditions most of those slaves originally came with and the American black family became one of oral traditions. Entire family histories were shared through stories, not by writing it all down. Thus, if Miss Lilla had died or lived an unusual life, somebody would have made it part of the family history, and Sebastian would have known more on the subject than he told me."

Though still ruffled, Leon gave a single nod. "Okay, then. We've got a window of time to look into. It's probably safe to assume she lived in or near Winston-Salem; otherwise, what was the point of hiring you?"

"Maybe I'm really that good."

"You are good. But I don't know about *that* good."

Max grinned. "Guess I'll comb through the local papers from that time and see what turns up."

"We got most of it here on microfilm. Some's been digitized, too. So you can run a few computer searches first. I want to go through some more of what we've got here."

"Thanks," Max said and offered his hand. Leon accepted and as they shook, he chuckled. Max laughed. "I know. I'm nuts, but I appreciate you helping me out despite all that."

After an hour had passed sitting in front of the microfilm viewer, Max's eyes burned and his neck had a crick in it. When he finally stumbled onto a reference to Miss Lilla, he had to read the article three times before he believed that he had not misread it. Each time through produced the same result — he had found her. He printed the article and rushed to find Leon.

The KKK's nightly activities had reached a fever pitch. Several papers had taken to writing regular articles about the hangings and burnings, and no matter how bad the state of twenty-four hour news often felt, the papers of the 19th century held little in check. Graphic photos of black bodies hanging from the trees accompanied most articles as well as lists of those who had gone unaccounted for. While reviewing those lists, Max had spotted the name *Lilla* one column over. He pointed it out to Leon.

With a careful eye, Leon read over the article. Max observed his friend's eye hover over the photograph. It depicted three bodies dangling from a tree while several white cloaked men stood and watched. One of the bodies looked particularly small.

When Max had seen the photo the first time, he processed it as a bit of research, a moment in history — despicable, grotesque, but no different than any harsh image on a television show. Leon's hesitation, however, drove the reality deep into Max's chest. These were real people that had been hung.

They might have been sleeping that night — parents and their child — when the glass windows shattered and the door broke down. Voices shouted at them as men rampaged into their home. Dressed like ghosts, they swarmed the sleeping family, dragged them outside, ignored their cries and pleas, assaulted them with kicks and punches, until the coarse ropes scraped their skin and lifted them into the air.

"Why do you stay here?" Max asked.

"What do you mean?" Leon asked, but they both knew what he had meant. "Where am I to go?"

"North? West? Any place without such a history for hating black people."

Leon looked up at Max as if catching a man running down the street naked while singing the British national anthem. "White people hate black people all over this country. It's better than it was back then, but the problem hasn't gone away. I stay in the South because this is my home, it's where I'm from. But I'll tell you something more. I got my degree in library sciences up in Pennsylvania. Beautiful state. Nice people. You know the town of Ephrata? Grand Wizard of the KKK lived there."

"I didn't mean to imply there were no bigots anywhere in the North, but I would think —"

"You would, but you'd be wrong. There are the same number of bigots everywhere. Difference here is that in the South, they aren't afraid to show their true colors. I know exactly who my friends are and who are my enemies down here. Up North, everyone smiles and treats you real nice. Until you leave and they start counting the silverware. So, no thank you. I'm happy to stay here. I know where I stand. I know who my people are."

Max didn't know if he bought Leon's idea as a constant truth, but he certainly could see how it held true for Leon. He simply didn't know enough black people to judge if all felt the same way. *And what's that say about me? That I don't know enough black people?*

Troubled by his thoughts, Max welcomed a change when Leon tapped the paper and said, "Hmmm. It says here that a family of three was hanged because the Ku Klux said they had attempted escape during the War. 'Governor Holden has requested the aid of Federal soldiers in calming the nightly agitations. This is good news to most Negroes who have been complaining about ill treatment. Miss Lilla H. was willing to be quoted as saying "We ain't slaves no more." This reporter agrees but notes that while Negroes are no longer slaves, that doesn't give them the mental faculties necessary for voting or participating in our civilized mode of life.' See that? There's still too many today who would agree with this paper."

"Racism issues aside, do you think that's Miss Lilla?"

Leon read the article again, his distaste for it pulsing off his tense shoulders and set jaw. At length, he nodded. "It could be her. It would explain a lot, too. See they call her 'Miss Lilla H.' which suggests that she's no slave."

"Civil War's over by this point. Nobody's a slave."

"I mean if she had been a slave, she'd have the Master's last name, or like Freeman, she would have changed it. Instead, the paper only gives her an initial. It's possible she was never a slave. That the letter stands for whatever her real last name is, and that the white men running the paper didn't want to acknowledge that but also wanted to make sure the KKK knew who to target for saying anything at all. Don't forget, the KKK was made up of all types — ex-soldiers, former slave owners, and plenty of people longing for the 'good old days' — so, they use the initial of her last name."

Max frowned. "That can't be the big secret. I mean, somebody killed Sebastian. Almost a hundred fifty years later, why would it matter if Lilla was a slave or not? It couldn't matter enough to kill a man. Could it?"

As Leon shrugged, Max's cell phone rang — Sandra. "Hi, hon," he said, enjoying the warm feeling of speaking to her with affection.

Instead of a warm response, Sandra's filled his ear with excited energy. "I've got him. I think I know why Sebastian was murdered."

Chapter 8

MAX MET UP WITH SANDRA AND DRUMMOND at the McDonald's across the street from their trailer park. They knew they shouldn't splurge on dinner out — even dinner as cheap as McDonald's — but none could stand the thought of discussing the case that evening while surrounded by their failure. At least while eating fast food, they could face the other direction and pretend that crappy trailer didn't await their return. More importantly, the restaurant had much better heating.

As Max and Sandra settled in on the same side of a booth, Max grabbed a fry. "So, tell me everything. Who killed Sebastian?"

Drummond slipped into the seat opposite them. "Hold on, there. Leed and I have spent the whole day in the Other, and I think we have some worthwhile information to provide."

"Don't you think knowing who killed Sebastian trumps anything you or I found?"

"First off, it wasn't just me. You keep forgetting Leed and he doesn't like it."

"Sorry," Max said, hoping the other diners ignored that he and Sandra appeared to be talking to each other yet looking across at an empty side of the booth. "I only forget sometimes because I can't see him."

"He says it's no big deal. What is big, though, is that we couldn't find Sebastian. I don't mean that we're narrowing in on him or that we got a clue. I mean, he isn't in the Other. I don't think he's dead."

"I saw his body. Heck, you saw his body."

"We saw *a* body. But I'm telling you he's not in the Other."

Sandra said, "Maybe he moved on. You know, like you were supposed to do."

"Only problem with that idea is that we know he hired Max to look into his family. Only a few things normally keep a ghost hanging around. Shocking death where the soul isn't willing to accept that the body is dead — that could easily apply if he had been murdered the way Max and I saw at Baxter House. But then finding him in the Other should have been a snap. Trust me, it's not hard to locate people who can't admit they're dead. They stand out."

"So, you don't think he died in a shock. That doesn't mean he's still alive."

"Another reason to stay is when you got unfinished business. Anybody murdered would have loads of unfinished business. I'm talking serious business here, not unpaid bills or something. I'm talking telling a loved one something very important along the lines of 'Gee, honey, you have a child I never told you about.' That kind of thing."

Max said, "Now, he didn't die or if he did, he's all good with his personal affairs?"

"Here's the kicker — a big reason ghosts stay around is when they are deeply disconnected from their lives. Sebastian Freeman hired us to find his relatives. He was searching for that kind of connection and never got it. So, if he were murdered, he most definitely would be haunting the area. I can't believe he would be allowed to move on with all this hanging over him."

"Well, he is dead. If he were alive, he would have called me by now." Max pointed a fry at Drummond. "And don't tell me he's faked his own death. I'm not buying that one."

"Stranger things have happened."

Sandra put down her burger. "Can we get to what I found?"

"Of course. Sorry, your husband can get so carried away."

Sandra lifted an eyebrow at Drummond. "I looked into two parts of this and found some very interesting things. First, I checked out Baxter House." Sandra had once been a Realtor and still had contacts in that world. They often provided her with information that she shouldn't have access to — her father had always said that it paid to maintain friendships.

"The house dates back to 1912 when a man named Cal Baxter inherited a tremendous sum of money. Several million dollars — which in 1912 was something like a hundred million today. He built the house that same year. Before becoming wealthy, he worked as a clerk for the local papers and his name never turned up in much else. After building the house, though, neighbors complained about strange noises and Baxter's unsociable behavior."

"1912?" Max tapped his chin in thought. "Did you find any mention of a woman named Lilla H?"

"No."

"She would have been quite old by then — especially for those times. Maybe 70."

Sandra shook her head. "Nobody like that came up, but I was only going through the Realtor's history, so I can't tell if he had children or if he was married or anything like that. None of that would show up in business papers from that time period since only men counted back then."

Max thought about what he had learned earlier that day, things Leon had said. If Lilla had never been a slave, she would have been making a living somehow before the war. And afterwards, all black people needed to find jobs. It was a chaotic time. But she would have had years of work experience under her belt. Getting a job might have been easier, but not necessarily easy — no matter what, she was still a black woman in the late 1860s looking for a job.

"Maybe," Max said, drawing out the word as he formulated his thoughts, "Lilla's child worked for Cal Baxter. Lilla would have probably been a highly sought after maid. One of the best in the area. If she wasn't a slave, she would have been better educated — at least enough to take care of herself and keep employed."

Drummond agreed. "Over time she builds up a good reputation and then trains her daughter to do the same. Did she have a daughter?"

"Lilla and Walter Freeman had two daughters and three sons. So, it's possible. By the time Cal Baxter has built his mansion, he hires the Freeman daughter to run the place based on the firm reputation of the mother."

Sandra pulled out her cell phone and tapped away. Their phones would be one of the last things to give up. Their trailer had no Internet connection, so they relied on their phones to stay connected to the world. "I'm making a note to look further into that. I'll see what I can find."

"I still don't see how all this Cal Baxter stuff tells us who murdered Sebastian."

"Patience, honey." Sandra finished her note and put the phone away. "After I found out the Baxter info, I turned my focus toward Luther Boer, and let me tell you this — he's lucky to still have his job. The Boer's are heavily in debt. They spent the last few months house hunting but couldn't secure a loan. I called their landlord and told her I was the bank following up their loan application. She told me they were two months behind on their rent."

"What a wonderfully sneaky move," Drummond said.

"I'm learning a lot hanging around you two. I also posed as a Realtor and was able to get access to the rest of their finances."

"Wait," Max said, his jaw as wide open as his eyes. "You can do that?"

"Oh, honey, it's easy. The world pretends we're all security conscious, but things are as loose as they ever were. Maybe even more than before computers."

She put her hand over his, and the simple gesture warmed him. "Luther's broke," he said. "Worse off than us. And he's got all sorts of problems because of that. I'm guessing you think he killed Sebastian."

"Doesn't it seem likely?"

Max thought for a moment. "We need more information. This is all good stuff, and I feel in my gut that we're closing in on things, but it's not there yet."

Rising in the air, Drummond said, "Okay, pal. What do you

want us to do?"

"You and Leed have got to find Sebastian."

"I told you —"

"He didn't fake his death, and you know it. So go back to the Other and find him, or find out where he went. While you're at it, see if you can find Cal Baxter in there. Maybe he'll tell us if he ever hired Lilla H's daughter. Sandra, I need you to do the same incredible job you just pulled finding information on Luther Boer, and go find whatever you can on Sebastian Freeman. I've been spending all my time looking into his past, but we don't know anything about his present."

"You can count on it," Sandra said. "What about you?"

"I've got to take on what might be the most dangerous job of all. I'm going to visit Luther Boer's wife."

Chapter 9

THE NEXT DAY, Max drove out east on Route 40 and exited onto Thomasville Road. The Winston-Salem city line ran clear out to the town of Walburg where there were several groups of apartment buildings. Some looked well-maintained and pricey. Others looked as if they had been designed in the 1970s — all brick and utilitarian. Then there were those that made Max thankful for his crappy trailer.

Pulling up to one of these disheveled buildings, Max noted the dented cars and scattered trash in the yards. In warmer weather, he imagined most of the people hung around outside — indoors would be too hot. But winter had arrived early, and the biting chill hit Max every time he got out of his car.

Knocking on the door to Apartment B, Max skipped from foot to foot and blew warm air on his hands. He had waited until Luther left for work, and he knew Luther's wife, Maria, was still inside. So, he knocked again. "Mrs. Boer? Please answer the door."

When the door finally opened, Max faced a short but harsh-looking white woman. With a cigarette in hand, scraggly hair tied back with a dirty kerchief, and eyes that didn't want to be bothered, she glared at him like a petulant teenager. "What do you want?"

"You're Mrs. Luther Boer?"

"Yeah?"

"I was hoping you could answer a few questions about your husband's involvement with the police department's crime scene division."

Her face lost all of its swagger. Jabbing her cigarette in his direction, she said, "I am not going through all that crap again.

You IAD people can talk to him direct. And he ain't dirty, so there ain't nothing to talk about anyways."

Max smiled and decided to play along. "No, no, ma'am, you misunderstand. We're not investigating your husband for any wrongdoing."

"You're not?"

"I promise you, he's not in any trouble coming from us. But he is involved in a case that has crossed our table regarding another officer, and I hoped by speaking with you, I might be able to get the information I need without causing your husband any embarrassment at headquarters. Those things can stall a career, and frankly, when it comes to IAD asking the questions, other police officers might make poor assumptions."

Her brow furrowed tight. "You sayin' that by talking with me, you're trying to protect him from getting an ass-whooping from the other cops?"

"Yeah, that's pretty much what I'm saying."

"Shit, why didn't you say so? Come on in." She walked away from him and headed into the kitchen. "Want a beer?"

Max glanced at his watch — 10:14 am. "I can't. I'm on duty."

The apartment stank of mold and grease. Max suspected the windows had never been opened, and the grime coating the bottoms of the panes backed up this idea. A torn couch sat against one wall and off to the side was a plastic table with two chairs. Junk mail piled up on the chairs, and the table looked like a dumping ground for pizza boxes and take out. In front of the couch was a stained coffee table with three full ashtrays. A few feet away, a small television perched on a pile of old phone directories. Behind the television, hung on the wall bold and proud, Max saw a large poster of a black fist.

Sauntering over to the couch, Maria took a swig from a beer bottle. "So, Mister IAD who don't want a beer, what is it you want to ask me?"

"I was interested in Luther's family history."

"Huh?"

"You see, the person I'm looking into has a long history in

this area going back all the way to the days when the land your home is on was probably a plantation. How far does Luther's family go back around here?"

With her mouth drawn tight, Maria set her beer on the coffee table. She stared at that beer, nodding to herself, and then stood. "Mister, we're good people and we don't deserve you trying to drag us down because of things that got nothing to do with us. We're down far enough as it is."

"I'm not trying to cause you trouble."

"Bullshit. I can hear it in your voice. You ain't good people. I seen the way you looked at that poster. You think you know everything and you've got your nose in the air about my home. Ever since y'all found out about Chicken, you been harassing us. Why you always giving Luther the shit jobs? Huh? Why you always passing over him for promotions? You ever think that maybe we need that money to survive? Pay him so little, work him all hours, and then you dare come here trying to paint us with a brush because ol' Chicken is in my past. Look around here. You think a top man in the police should be living like this?"

"I apologize, ma'am. I'm not insinuating anything about you or your husband. I really only wanted to ask a few questions."

"Well, you ain't asked anything yet, but you sure implying a lot."

Max closed his mouth. Part of him wanted to ask her what Luther had told her he did for a living or about Luther's gambling. Part of him thought that was too vindictive and might cause trouble for him down the road. Still another part argued that she had a right to know the truth about her husband. Except, other parts of him pointed out, it wasn't his place to provide that truth.

Turning to leave, Maria said, "Figures. Y'all are such pansies. Can't solve a crime without Luther but you want to hang him every time he speaks the truth about racial problems."

Max halted and turned back. "Your husband spends his days collecting evidence at crime scenes for others to process. It's not a high level position. And the reason you're poor isn't his job. Even the lowest crime tech makes good money. Luther's just a fool who gambles it all away instead of sharing it with you." The words were out of his mouth before he could stop himself.

"Get out," she growled. Then she lunged at Max, pounding his back with her fists. "Get out of here! Don't you ever come back!"

Driving home, Max thought over all Leon had said about people being more honest and straight-forward down here, and in regards to the subject of prejudice, he had to agree. It was easier in the South to know where people stood.

More importantly for the case, Maria Boer's lack of filter on her thoughts led to her letting the word *Chicken* slip. Whatever that referred to, Max knew he wouldn't end up researching poultry.

The work went fast. Searching the name Chicken with North Carolina and the late-1800s gave him all he needed. By the time he sat across from Sandra and sipped on his instant noodle soup, he had plenty to share.

"Back during the Reconstruction," Max said, "there was a man named John Walter 'Chicken' Stephens. He got the name when he was young because he stole chickens. Anyway, after the war, he was a Republican as well as a lapdog to the Governor — a scalawag who aided the KKK by turning a blind eye to their actions."

Sandra nibbled on a piece of toast — the other extravagant part of their meal. "I thought the Republicans of that time became the Democrats of today."

"Sort of. And the Democrats back then were also the Conservative party. It gets confusing. It also doesn't matter as much because the bigotry ran deep on all sides. Chicken Stephens didn't care what party he was with as long as it benefited him. Though nobody could outright prove it, he was suspected of burning barns that belonged to black families, and there were even accusations of murder. Oh and most people of the time, including members of the press, took it as a given that Stephens had stolen his seat in the North Carolina Senate."

"What a lovely man."

"After meeting the woman Luther Boer married, I have little doubt she's related. Must've been quite a shock when he found out."

"Probably caused his gambling problem."

"Anyway, in May of 1870, the Democrats were holding a convention in the Caswell County Courthouse to figure out their plans for the August state elections. Chicken walks right into the Courthouse despite death threats to him and his family. Even his niece stopped him on his way to warn him that trouble was brewing. But he carried three guns whenever he left the house, so he didn't think he had to worry."

"Sounds like he should have worried."

"You know it. He goes into the courthouse which is filled with former Confederate soldiers and politicians. Nearly three hundred. He runs into Frank Wiley, the county sheriff, and asks him to run again but for the Republican Party. Wiley says he'll decide later, and in a few hours, Chicken gets a note from Wiley saying they should talk. So, Chicken's probably thinking that things are going great for him. He meets Wiley and they go to a small storeroom out behind the courthouse."

Sandra snorted. "Because there's nothing suspicious with that."

"Don't forget. Chicken had ignored a bunch of death threats and because of his connection to the governor, he held a lot of power. I think he was so cocky, he never imagined anyone could touch him."

"But they did, right?"

"Of course. When Wiley and Chicken got in the storeroom, there were three other men waiting. Wiley ducks out and the three men, with the help of a few others, murdered Chicken. Hung and stabbed him."

"And this guy's related to Maria Boer?"

Max finished his soup but his stomach still felt empty. "Yeah, but I think there's a deeper connection to this case. See, in addition to being a prick, Chicken pissed people off because he also worked with the Union League. They were a very private society that organized former slaves to vote together as a political group — specifically for the Republican party. Since that was Lincoln's party, most black voters sided with the Republicans, anyway, but through the Union League, these former slaves created the backbone for the party in North Carolina. The League also fought back against the KKK, playing out their own violent missions most nights. The war was officially over, but each night the streets were a madhouse of vengeance."

"I think I see where this is going. Lilla, right?"

"Exactly. Since Chicken Stephen was active with the Union League, there's a possibility that he came into contact with either Lilla or her husband."

Sandra leaned forward, her eyes blazing with excitement. "That's real interesting because it ties in with what I learned today about Baxter House."

Drummond poked his head through the ceiling. "Sounds like I got here at the right time."

"Not exactly," Max said. "You missed me telling all that I found out about Chicken Stephens."

"Now it really sounds like I got here at the right time."

Sandra winked at Drummond, and he gave a bashful grin back. "Can I tell about Baxter House now, or do you two still have some bickering to do?"

"The floor is yours," Drummond said with a bow and he settled near the sink.

"Thank you. Most of what I found on Sebastian was pretty mundane. He was a local, which we knew, and he went to Reynolds high school. Got a liberal arts degree from UNC and seems to have stayed around Winston-Salem ever since. I'm not completely sure, though, because he jumped from address to address — sometimes more than twice in a year — and then not at all. See, once he's out of college, records of him become rather sparse. No employment records, no W-2s, nothing like that. He didn't pay his taxes at all. In fact, I can't even find where he lived in the last few years."

"Was he one of those 'off-the-grid' types?" Max asked.

"Seems that way. Except then about a year ago, he applies for a position cleaning and taking care of Baxter House. I can't find anything that suggests he looked for any other job. He sought out that specific job and only that job."

"That's definitely strange. I don't know what it means though."

Drummond said, "It means he had a specific reason for wanting access to that house. He didn't need the job for money or anything. Just access."

"But what if he never got the job? What if it went to somebody else?"

"Lots of options — depends on how far he was willing to go. Before the job went elsewhere, he could threaten the other applicants, make them back out. Or, if that didn't work, he could create a new job opening by killing off the guy with the position he wants. There's also bribery. Or he could look into his employer's history, find something damaging, and blackmail his way into the position. That's just off the top of my head."

Max wagged a finger at Drummond. "You think in a very twisted way."

"See how your mind works once you've been at this as long as I have."

Sandra raised her voice. "Boys, stop it and listen." She let them stare at each other for a few seconds before continuing. "It doesn't matter how he did it because the fact is that he did it. Sebastian Freeman got that job. So, I looked into Baxter House and found some important things. After Cal Baxter came into his money, he had the place built quickly, paying double what it was worth to make sure it was done fast. He also designed the house himself and kept the number of workers to a minimum. Even weirder — he had large wood fences built around the property until construction was done."

"So nobody knows what exactly was built except what we see now."

"Right."

Drummond clicked his tongue. "That doesn't bode well for the builders."

Max nodded. "Sadly, I agree with you."

"You two." Sandra shook her head. "The builders were fine. No mysterious deaths or anything like that. They simply were paid a lot of money to stay silent, and they did."

"See that," Drummond said. "Bribery. The choice of the non-violent."

"After Baxter moves in, everything in the neighborhood is quiet. And then he dies. He was a young man, mid-thirties, in good health. No sign of foul play. His maid found him dead in his study."

Max's skin prickled. "Just like Sebastian."

"Baxter had no heirs. Even if he had, the whole estate was a mess. He had come into this money unexpectedly and didn't know much about managing such a large sum, so he never got around to making a formal will. Baxter House went up for auction, and guess what local family outbid everyone, paying nearly twice the house's worth at the time."

"Don't say it."

"Sorry, Hon, but you know it's coming — Hull. And like we all know and love with the Hulls, after purchasing the house, all mention of the house vanishes from that point forward. My opinion on all of this — Cal Baxter had something the Hulls wanted. Whatever it is, it's still in the house. Sebastian found out about it and took that job so he could search the house over and over."

Max perked up. "If Sebastian got close to finding it, the Hulls wouldn't be too happy. They have him killed and make sure Luther Boer is the crime tech on the scene. They use him to corrupt the evidence, making sure the murder doesn't tie back to them. Luther's dead broke. As Drummond would happily point out, he needs money and a bribe would be an easy way for the Hulls to clean up the mess."

Bringing his hands together in one sharp clap, Drummond said, "You both know what this means we've got to do, right?"

"No," Max said, pushing back his chair. "There's no need to go breaking into that house."

"Are you serious? There's every need. If the Hulls murdered

Sebastian, then it means he had gotten close to finding out what they're hiding. If someone else murdered Sebastian, then it means the murderer is getting close. Either way, the Hulls are smart enough to know that Baxter House is no longer a safe place to hide whatever it is they're hiding. As soon as the police release the house, the Hulls are going to send somebody in there to clean the place out. Frankly, it's taken us so long to figure this much out, it may be too late already. So, there's no other way around it. We've got to go tonight."

Max turned to Sandra but she raised her hands. "Don't look at me. I agree with the dead guy."

Drummond flicked the front of his hat. "Thanks, Doll."

"Fine," Max said with plenty of snap. "Let's at least wait until midnight or so, and maybe we can actually plan ahead this time. That might be a new and exciting approach for us."

"No need to get snippy."

"I swear there better not be a witch sitting there, waiting for us. I'm sick of witches."

Chapter 10

BY THE TIME THEY PUT TOGETHER A PLAN, got some rest, gathered together the few things they needed, and drove to the ritzy part of town, the next day had begun. Max parked the car a block over from Baxter House and checked the clock — 1:02 am. The street looked like the set of a strange movie where everyone had been quarantined — empty and silent, the cars safely stowed in their driveways, no movement, only a handful of lights on, and the blue flicker of a television.

Both Max and Sandra had dressed in dark clothing, and as she checked their equipment bag, Max had to chuckle. "I swear it looks like we're cat burglars."

"We can always consider that to be our back up plan if we end up dead broke."

Drummond poked his head between them. "With my help, you guys would be great at it. But there's that whole criminal element problem. Namely, that I'm not a criminal element."

"Relax," Sandra said. "We're just joking."

Max frowned. "What's the matter?" he asked Drummond.

Drummond gazed out the window. "Nothing. Got a weird feeling, that's all. Don't worry about it. But keep alert. Let's go."

As they walked toward Baxter House, the temperature dropped around them. Max's nose froze up and he chastised himself for not bringing a warmer coat. Thick clouds obscured the moon.

Sandra said, "It's supposed to ice over tonight."

Max nodded. "I don't know if I'll ever get used to North Carolina winter. We get maybe two snowfalls that are gone before ten o'clock the next day but plenty of ice storms that screw up the mornings for everyone, knocking down trees, and cutting wires. It's crazy."

"Then let's not take too long with this. I don't want to be driving back on ice."

The house loomed ahead — darker against the moonless sky. Their footsteps amplified in their ears as they stepped onto the property. Max paused.

"Why are we always doing this stuff at night?" he asked. "We're smart. We could've come up with some reason to check out the house during the day."

Drummond said, "You're not looking too smart with that question. Sneaking around at night goes with the job. Less people to notice you. Less trouble to deal with."

"Besides," Sandra said, "we deal with ghosts, and ghosts prefer the cold and the dark of night. Most do, anyway."

"And it's more fun this way. So quit complaining and get ready. I'll go open the door." Drummond whisked off to the house.

Max opened their bag and pulled out two flashlights. Handing one to Sandra, he said, "It was a rhetorical question."

"I know." She kissed him on the cheek. "You're cute. Now, let's get inside. It'll be warmer."

Drummond unlocked the front door, and they slipped under the yellow police crime scene tape. Max flicked on his flashlight and its beam created stark shadows throughout the foyer. Even in the dark, the night had transformed Baxter House into a sinister looking place, but the constant shifting of shadows caused by the moving flashlights sent chills along Max's arms.

The plan they had devised consisted of Max and Sandra splitting up to cover the house as fast as possible. With Drummond available between them, a simple shout would bring him in to help — the only reason they were willing to split up at all. They also hoped the search would go quickly because they weren't going to be looking at any place obvious.

Something hidden as long as this had been would not be sitting in a drawer or behind a safe. Nor would it be in a secret drawer behind a false back or a secret safe behind a painting.

Such things would have been discovered by now — especially with Sebastian having had plenty of time to search.

Sandra dug into their bag and pulled out two walkie-talkies. She checked that they had been set to the same channel, then handed one to Max. Watching her climb the foyer stairs to search the second floor, Max crossed his fingers — he hoped they had not made a huge mistake. He then hurried through the door on the left. He entered a sitting room filled with heavy furniture, a fireplace, a small bar, and several portraits on the walls. Playing the flashlight against the walls, he looked for any sign of a false panel. He checked the floor and ceiling as well. Nothing looked out of place.

He moved on down a hall that led to the kitchen. Though he had been in the kitchen before, it looked quite different at night and coming in from an alternate angle. Plus, his previous experience involved loads of police and trepidation. He had plenty of the latter, but without the police the room appeared longer and more spacious.

A creaking sound echoed around him. Max froze — his heart pounding. The creak came again — Sandra walking above. Releasing his held breath, he wiped his forehead.

As with the sitting room, Max checked over the walls, floor, and ceiling. He looked at the depth of the room and made sure it matched up with the hall he had walked through. It matched. Had it come up short, he would have suspected a secret room.

"This is going to take a long time," he muttered.

Drummond swooped in from the closed study door. "Found it," he said.

"Already?"

"Not that hard considering how I found it."

They called Sandra down and entered the study. Max halted in the doorway, his eyes locked on the floor. Sebastian's body had been moved to the city morgue, but Max could still see him — not his ghost but rather an after image burned in the back of Max's memory. It clung to the floor and the walls and the desk and even the air. It coated the room with an awful foreboding as if at any moment, flames would burst out and consume them all. Sebastian's ghost would have been easier to take.

Sandra looked back. "You feel it, too?"

Max managed a slight nod.

"Over here," Drummond said, standing next to the wall opposite the study desk.

Max took one step into the room, then opted to use his flashlight on the wall rather than walk further in. "Looks like a wall. What am I missing?"

"This," Drummond said, leaning his body against the wall. "I can't pass through it here. There's a room on the other side of this wall. I can pass through the walls all around it, but I can't get in."

Sandra reached out and cautiously touched the wall. "I don't feel anything strange, but clearly there's a ward on this room to keep out ghosts. Possibly other supernatural things, as well."

"Right, but there's still got to be a way to open it up. A book to pull or a button to press. Nobody would make a room without a way in. Would they?"

Intrigued, Max edged further in. "The Hulls might. They certainly are capable of casting this ward that's got you blocked. If they're trying to hide something, what better way to do it than have no access to it?"

"Guess we should've brought an ax or a sledgehammer."

They all searched the study for any kind of mechanism to unlock a way in — just in case. Books were tilted outward and furniture moved. Max checked out the desk extensively and found nothing but empty drawers.

"Oh, are we ever stupid," Sandra said and sat on the edge of the desk.

"Not you," Drummond said. "Just Max."

Sandra pulled out her cell phone and tapped away. "We know there's a room and that there's a ward on the wall. That tells us a lot. The presence of a ward means the presence of magic. In particular, this all tells us that there won't be a secret lever that opens a secret door. Max is half-right when he said the Hulls would build a room with no access. See, they built a room with no regular access, but magic access — that's a different matter entirely."

"Sounds good." Max sidled up next to her and peeked at her phone. "What are you looking up?"

"Magic spells. Ever since we started dealing with witches, I've been surfing the web for quality sites about magic. It's taken awhile — there's a ton of crap out there to sift through."

"You expected different? It's the Internet."

"Except the keyword *magic* can go to a lot of different subjects. There are all kinds of groups that pretend they know magic. There's also people who play the card game, Magic. The word also links to people who perform entertainment magic or write about magic or write fiction involving magic. It goes on and on. But I've found a handful of sites that I trust."

Max nudged her shoulder. "Are you going to learn to be a witch now?"

"Maybe." Not the answer he wanted, but she kept her focus on the cell phone. "I haven't decided about that yet. But if we keep getting deeper into this kind of thing, it might be helpful if one of us learns a few spells, at the least." Smiling, she tapped her phone. "Got it."

Sandra approached the wall with her hand out. She pressed her palm against the wood and checked her phone one more time. After reading through the information, she put the phone in her pocket.

"What can we do to help?" Drummond asked.

"Nothing, thanks." She licked her finger and drew a circle around the hand on the wall. Another lick, and she drew a symbol above the circle — one Max had seen before. He jumped to his feet, his mouth unable to work properly as he stared at the symbol. He had seen it at the fights — glowing on the hand of an old witch.

"Honey, I don't think —"

Lightning flashed inside the room, the walls shook with a thunderous explosion, and Sandra flew backward, crashing into the bookshelves. Books tumbled out and fell on her. Max hurried behind the desk to help her up.

"Are you hurt bad? Can you hear me? Honey?"

Sandra sat up, her head weaving as if drunk. "Did it work?" she said, her voice sounding stronger than the way she looked.

Max peered over the desk. He expected to see a burnt out hole in the wall with splintered bits of wood hanging like sickly teeth. Instead, he saw a finely-crafted door — mahogany with white marble inlays and gold hardware. "Did you make that?"

"No. It was there the whole time. My spell simply revealed the door."

They waited a few minutes until Sandra could stand without help. Then, they approached the door together. Drummond stopped behind them.

"I can't get any closer," he said. "It's like trying to walk through a wall — and that wall spits out little shocks to boot."

Max put his hand on the doorknob. "Stay there, then. But if you can peek through the doorway, that'd be good."

"See that — you do like having me here to watch out for you."

"I just don't want to have to tell you everything that goes on in there."

"Sure. I understand." Drummond crossed his arms, cocked his head to the side, and smiled.

Max opened the door. With Sandra leaning on his shoulder, they walked inside. Fluorescent lights flickered on from above. One buzzed loudly and flickered off.

In what light remained, Max saw a circular room with heavy stone walls like a medieval castle turret. Seven doorways had been carved into the walls, but even from the study, Max could see that the doors would never open — they were merely carvings of doors, not doors themselves. To the left hung a portrait of a stern man with little hair and bushy white eyebrows. He seemed to be staring at the center of the room, which made sense to Max considering the painted circle on the floor complete with numerous magic symbols. A four-foot candlestick stood in the center of the circle and a black, unlit candle perched at the top.

Sandra walked over to the portrait to inspect the metal plate underneath. "Says this is Cal Baxter."

"Kind of an ugly guy," Max said as he squatted near the circle. He ran a finger along the paint, curious if it was so old it would flake off or so new his fingers might stick.

Something heavy smacked into his head. He saw splotches of color and his ears rang. He heard huffing like a bull ready to charge. And he saw a creature with ram's horns and a flat face — its nose and eyes and mouth mere suggestions of flesh slit open.

"Max!"

Sandra's voice.

His eyes fluttered open. He lay on the floor of the study. "What happened?"

Drummond peered out the window. "You passed out. What do you think happened?"

"Can you stand?" Sandra asked.

"Don't coddle him. You two have got to get moving. A car pulled up. Somebody's getting out. Oh, crap, it's Rolson."

Sweat beaded on Max's forehead and his body chilled. He sat up. The motion caused his stomach to constrict, but he managed to avoid throwing up. With Sandra's help, he struggled to his feet.

"First you dropped, then me. What happens if we both go?" He tried to smile, but all humor fled when he saw Rolson standing in the doorway to the hall.

"Well, bless your heart," Rolson said in a dead voice. "Y'know, when I heard a call came in from a concerned neighbor that somebody had broken into the Baxter House, I knew it was you. I even told the beat cops I'd handle it — that's how confident I was that when I walked in here, I'd find you. Didn't expect you to bring your wife, though."

Trying to stand straight, Max said, "This isn't what you think. We're not trying to steal anything."

"I didn't think you were." Rolson stared straight at Max, the corners of his mouth twitching as if he held back a sadistic grin. "If anything, I figure you wanted to get rid of some evidence we must have missed. Or to show off to the missus the scene of your crime."

"My crime? You don't really think I —"

"Let me make this clear to you — as in crystal clear and five-by-five. I warned you not to cross my path again. I told you it would be a bad move. See, I've found that there are two types that don't follow a solid warning like that — idiots and criminals. Which one are you?"

"I'm not a criminal, so I guess you think I'm an idiot." Max took a breath, ready to launch into a verbal assault regarding his rights and justice and how come he's the only one looking seriously into Sebastian Freeman's murder, when he felt Sandra's hand grip his waist tight. No need to look at her. Max knew the expression in her eyes and the thought in her head — *Keep your mouth shut.*

Drummond drifted into the room. Max hadn't realized the ghost had left. "I checked outside. Rolson's alone. That's not a good sign."

Rolson sauntered into the study. He rolled his knuckles on the desk as he looked around. "I can see how it played out in here. You were hired to look into Freeman's ancestry, right?"

Max nodded. He tried to be aware of whatever danger they were in — Drummond certainly worried — yet part of his thoughts couldn't help but wander off to another oddity. Why hadn't Rolson noticed the open door leading to a room with witchcraft on the floor?

"What did you find, Mr. Porter? What little bit of Freeman's history did you uncover that made him so mad?"

Drummond came in close behind Rolson. "You get what's happening? This guy's trying to pin the murder on you. Rich areas like this want their messy crimes cleaned up fast. He's probably under a lot of pressure to find a murderer, and you're the only one he's got."

"I told you the other day, I hadn't seen Sebastian. He hired me, and I went to work, but I hadn't really found anything yet."

"Oh, I'm not so sure about that." Rolson winked at Sandra as he walked back to the doorway. "I think you met him here while he worked an honest job, and you threatened to expose whatever you found out. I know you're not doing well. Plus you lost plenty gambling. Probably lost it that way before. A little blackmail money might've been just the thing you two needed to get back on your feet."

"That's not true."

"But Freeman refused to play along. He grew angry. Now, I'm not saying you killed him on purpose. This wasn't a premeditated thing. No, I've seen enough heat-of-the-moment crimes in my time and this one's a classic."

Max stepped forward, and Rolson's hand went underneath his jacket. Max froze. Rolson could have a gun or he could be bluffing. Either way it didn't matter. Max wasn't going to take the risk. Not with Sandra close enough to get clipped by accident.

Punctuating his words by pointing at the spot where the body had been found, Max said, "I did not kill Sebastian Freeman."

Rolson pulled out a silver handgun. "Of course, you did. Raise your hands and turn around. Maxwell Porter, you are under arrest for the murder of Sebastian Freeman." Sandra rushed to Max's side, but Rolson raised his gun. "There, there, little lady. Take a few steps back or you'll be spending time behind bars, too."

As Max started to turn away, Rolson's eyes bugged out and his mouth dropped. A second of confusion mixed with pain rushed across his face before he collapsed to the floor.

Drummond hurried over. "It wasn't me. I swear."

With his hands still in the air, Max stared at Rolson. "Is he dead? Did he have a heart attack?"

Sandra placed her fingers on Rolson's neck. "He's alive. And it didn't look like a heart attack to me. I thought for sure Drummond had given him a hard chill."

"Well, I didn't," Drummond said. "But I would've if things went any further."

Max lowered his hands and stared at the magic painted on the floor of the secret room. "Let's get out of here."

"What about him?" Sandra asked.

"I don't know. I guess he'll come after us when he wakes

up. But we don't want to be here, do we?"

"But then aren't we fugitives?"

Drummond shooed her away from Rolson. "Both of you should go. Don't worry about him coming after you. I promise you he won't be knocking on your door in the morning."

"But —"

"He wants to frame you for this murder, right? You go home and act normal. He can't claim you were running from the law if you don't really run. He still has to answer to his superiors, and not only would they wonder why you weren't actually on the run but acting normal instead, they'll want Rolson's evidence in the case, and he's got none. Here, he has you returning to the crime scene. He arrests you, you run and maybe he takes a shot, he says you confessed — something like that. Out of this house, he's got nothing. Not yet, at least. So, get out of here and you'll have bought a little time."

Sandra looked to Max. "He's right."

"I know," Max said. He saw the fear in her eyes and knew they only reflected his own fear.

Chapter 11

BY THE TIME MAX AND SANDRA had returned to their trailer, both were wired and unable to sleep. Every car that drove by sounded like the police. Max kept expecting the flashing lights and the short, sharp bursts of a siren followed by a knock at their door.

But nobody came. No car flashed its lights. They were left alone.

When day arrived with overcast gloom, Max decided to go to the library. "I've missed something important. I must have. Somewhere there's got to be a journal or a diary or a news article — something about Baxter House or Freeman. There's got to be."

Sandra agreed. "I'll help. We can double the chance of finding something."

"Good idea. Go find what more you can on Sebastian —"

"I meant I'll go to the library with you."

Max paused. He knew a marriage minefield when he saw one. Closing his eyes as if praying, he said, "I'd rather you didn't."

"Oh?" Sandra said, sounding like the click of a pressure switch.

"You're right that you'd be a great help, but the library to me is a private place. My place. Drummond doesn't even bother me there."

"So I'd be bothering you?"

"Don't twist what I say. Everybody has their little places of, I don't know, sanctuary. The library is mine. You don't need old books to find out what I'm asking of you. A laptop will do just fine. But I need the quiet, the feel, heck, the smell of a library as I'm going through diaries from a hundred-fifty years ago."

Sandra kissed him. "I know. I'm just giving you hard time. I'll call you if I find anything."

As Max drove off for Wake Forest University, he thought about what he had said. He had never put it in such clear words for himself but it rang true. The library was his sanctuary — private and, in a way, holy.

Yet he had allowed Leon to join, to help in the research. Why him and not Sandra?

"I suppose," Max said to the steering wheel as he drove over the speed bumps at the front of the University's property, "Leon shares that pure love of research with me." Could it be that simple? Leon understood a part of him that even his own wife failed to grasp — that research holds a Zen quality over him. It cleared the mind by letting all else drift away in order to focus on one task. At the same time, it reminded him of a puzzle, a mystery that demanded to be solved.

As he entered the library, he found it difficult to shed his uneasiness. The overcast day darkened the skylights and cast the entire library in a gloomy cloud. The rain would come soon, and the longer it waited, the worse it would be. Knowing that loomed over him felt like the growing pressure of knowing that Rolson had to be out there searching for some way to pin Sebastian's murder on him.

"Then stop moping and get researching," Max muttered and stomped upstairs to the Special Resources room.

He spent several hours looking through information about Baxter House and Sebastian Freeman, but what he could find (which did not amount to much) provided nothing new or useful. He needed to locate that one nugget which would clear his mind and let him see the situation in a fresh way. But after all the research he had done in the last few days, he knew he had found all that the library and the Internet could produce. An ugly sensation had formed in his gut, one that spelled the end for this job.

"No," he whispered. That would be fine for a simple

research project, but if he failed at this, he might be setting himself up for a jail sentence. "No *might* about it."

Stretching his arms over his head, Max decided to start at the top of his resource list and go through each one again. This time, he would pay particular attention to the little details and side notes. He had to have missed something.

Less than twenty minutes later, he found a reference to a short story published in the early 1900s. Nothing odd about that, but since he wanted to focus on the small things he had ignored previously, Max decided to find the story and see what it was about. He wrote down the necessary information and went to the help desk.

"Hi, Max," Leon said with a smile.

"Leon! I had no idea you were up here today."

"I'm always here. Just about live here." He chuckled. "I'm foolin'. Really I'm only filling in for a guy that got sick. This was supposed to be my day off. What can I do for you? You still looking into all that Sebastian Freeman stuff?"

"Yup. Found this, but I don't know if it's anything or not." Max handed over the slip of paper with the book request.

"Well, let's see what we see."

Three minutes later, Leon returned empty-handed but smiling. "That story was published in *The New York World Sunday Magazine* and we don't keep the originals anymore. But don't worry, this is a library. We're getting it all digitized now."

"So, where can I read it?"

"Follow me."

Leon brought Max to a computer terminal set up in a cubicle. A few taps at the keyboard, and the story appeared. Before Max sat next to Leon to read the piece, his heart jumped. On the screen he saw:

Kings of Dante
by Bill Sydney
for my friend, Cal Baxter

"Leon, this is what I've been looking for. Now, I've just got to find out who Bill Sydney is."

"That's easy. I already know. Bill Sydney is a pseudonym used by William Sydney Porter. He was a prolific short story writer and went by a lot of different names."

"Never heard of him."

"Sure you have. His most famous pseudonym was O. Henry."

Max's world skipped a frame. "Wait, what? William Sydney Porter is O. Henry? The writer? *Gift of the Magi.* That guy?"

"That's the one."

Max stared at the computer screen, the letters burning into his mind. O. Henry had dedicated a story to Cal Baxter. They knew each other.

"Guess I've got to go learn about O. Henry," Max said.

Leon patted him on the shoulder. "I know the perfect book."

True to his word, Leon provided Max with an excellent biography of O. Henry that went far in-depth into the man's life. Straight from the opening pages, Max knew this was the right nugget to follow because it turned out that O. Henry came from Greensboro, North Carolina.

Born in 1862 with the real name William Sydney Porter, he lived in Greensboro for much of his youth. Sharing the last name Porter barely registered in Max's mind. He had learned long ago that certain names, Porter among them, were so common that to get excited about a possible connection meant getting disappointed more often than not.

As William grew older, he spent his early adult years wandering around from job to job trying to find a place to fit in. He worked at his uncle's drugstore and earned his pharmacist license at nineteen. He sketched portraits of customers, and though the biography did not mention it specifically, Max thought it fairly certain that William tried to sell some of these sketches. Probably ticked off the uncle but not enough to get fired. Still, he ended up traveling down to Texas where he tried his hand working on a sheep ranch, doing everything from shepherding to cooking to entertaining —

somewhere along the line he had become a decent guitarist.

Max rolled his neck to relieve a sore spot when he noticed how dark the library had become. He checked his watch — 5:37 pm. Most people had left for the day. Leon had left and Max never even noticed. Later in the evening, students would fill up the space as they worked on papers and projects.

The sky grew darker while he sat there, and he considered packing up the books and going home. But the lure of his research overrode his desire to avoid driving in bad weather.

"When I'm done with the O. Henry book," he promised.

Sticking his head back into the book, Max worked diligently for two more hours. He might have continued until the library closed, but he heard something that stopped him — silence.

Not the quiet of a library, but a true absence of sound. No buzz of lighting. No hums of electricity. Not one fan blowing or heater pumping. Not a gentle murmur of conversation between the stacks or the soft click-clack of a librarian typing on a computer. Nothing. As if all the sound in the world had ceased.

Max's body stilled as his eyes searched the darkening library. He couldn't see far, though, due to the numerous rows of books and a few thick posts. On one post, a fire alarm hung. If he bolted for it right away, he could set it off and force everyone outside. But he didn't move. He didn't like the idea of taking such a bold action without knowing what he faced. For all he knew, the Hulls had sent a witch after him, and that person stood right behind the post he would be running for. He needed more information.

Off to his left, the stairwell doors flew open without a sound. The lights in the stairwell flashed sporadically. Max squinted, trying to make who had come. Not who, he saw — but what.

A large beast stepped forward like the Minotaur from the Greek myths. It hulked in the doorway, its massive shoulders covered in hair, long snout dripping with mucus, and thick muscles bulging with strength. Unlike the myths, though, this creature bore two ram's horns — one on either side of its head.

Ram's horn? Max recalled a flashing image from Baxter House. The creature turned its eyes — dark, cloudy eyes — upon Max.

Max's cell phone buzzed.

The sudden noise jolted him. He sat at the table, his heart racing, his mouth dry, as the quiet bustle of the library went on around him. He heard a librarian speaking with a student. He saw the well-lit stairs as two young women walked through — one accidentally bumping her large purse against the post that had no fire alarm but rather a taped-flier for the Drama Department's latest production of "No Exit".

Max's head felt stuffy as if he had been asleep. He wanted to accept that as the simple answer — he had dreamed while asleep. But it had felt real. Not the way a dream that feels real feels real but rather the way reality feels real. Because no matter how real a dream may seem, upon waking, the dream faded. Occasionally, the false reality of the dream lasted a short while, but no matter what, the dream faded. Otherwise, there would be people walking around unsure of whether they were asleep or awake. Max guessed there might be a few mentally ill people with that problem, but not him — he knew he had not been asleep.

The phone flashed the receiving of a text message. Max stared at it, knowing that once he moved his body, all sense of whatever had happened would fall apart. The full weight of the real world would crash down and destroy the delicate balance his head walked between real and possible-dream. *No,* he thought, *it couldn't have been a dream.* But it couldn't have been real either. Ghosts, witches, curses, two-hundred-year-old men, covens, even whatever Leed was — Max could accept all of that. He had experience it all. But a demon Minotaur? No. That went too far.

Max finally picked up the phone. As expected, the tactile sensation hardened reality around him. He had no idea what had happened, but he knew the phone with its message, that was reality. He glanced at the screen — Sandra.

He brought up the message. It read: *Found Freeman's house.* Then she gave an address in Greensboro.

Chapter 12

MAX DROVE ROUTE 40 TOWARDS GREENSBORO. From the library, he knew it would be around forty minutes which gave him time. He kept remembering that creature, the way it stared at him, the way it filled in the stairwell, the way it soaked up all sound.

Shaking off the memory, he called Sandra and set his phone on speaker. "Hi, hon. Great work. I'm heading out to Greensboro now," he said.

"It was nothing."

Despite his wracked emotions, he grinned. Sandra had worked hard to track down that address — once more proving how indispensable she was to this outfit. As with their marriage, they were a team in this business, and as with their marriage, only when they worked together did things ever turn out right.

"How'd your research go?" she asked.

His grin lifted to a full smile. She understood exactly why he had called. A forty-minute drive after tons of research — he needed to put all the pieces into place and she knew he thought best when he thought out loud. She had offered herself as a sounding board.

"What do you know about O. Henry?"

"The writer?"

"He wrote a story dedicated to Cal Baxter. To start with, O. Henry's real name is William Porter." Max went through the early years quick and got to the point where William headed down to Texas. "After a few more years bouncing around jobs, he got married and ended up in Austin working at the First National Bank. He was a lousy banker. For starters, he wasn't very careful with bookkeeping."

Sandra chuckled. "That seems like a major problem for a banker."

"Didn't help that he played rather loose with banking ethics. Not a problem if you're the CEO of Goldman Sachs."

"Not at all. You cheat the entire country and get a bailout."

"But when you're low man on the totem pole, and it's the 1890s, not so good for you. He was accused of embezzlement and fired. Weird thing though, they never indicted him."

"You think the bank made him take the fall for something they did?"

"Hold on, this gets messier. At this point, he moves his family to Houston. Some of the weekly dabbling he had done with writing caught the eye of an editor at the Houston Post. He went on to write for them regularly, and famously got a lot of his ideas by hanging out in hotel lobbies and eavesdropping. All seemed to be going fine until the First National Bank of Austin got audited. The Feds found out about the embezzlement and somebody had to take the fall. Now, get this part, this is crazy. His father-in-law posts his bail and a day before his trial, something clicks in him and he runs. Heads to New Orleans and then finds his way to Honduras. At that time, Honduras had no extradition treaty with the US, so he was safe."

"This is the guy who becomes O. Henry?"

"I know, it's amazing. All this is happening to him, and he's writing and getting stories published the whole time. And it might have gone on like that, but his wife was ill. She'd suffered from tuberculosis since before they were married, but now she was dying. So, he came back to Austin to see her and turned himself in. The father-in-law actually posted bail again, just so O. Henry could see his wife. In the end, he was sentenced to five years and shipped off to a prison in Ohio."

"But that's not the end for us."

"No. Because he continued to write stories, and as he had all along, he continued to get them published under numerous pseudonyms, but the O. Henry pseudonym had become the most popular — supposedly the name came from one of his favorite guards. For a handful of years in the early 1900s, he wrote hundreds of stories. It was incredible output. But in 1910, he died. He was a heavy drinker his whole life and it finally took its toll."

Sandra said, "So, how did he know Cal Baxter?"

"I haven't a clue." Max had reached the edge of Guilford County which meant the city of Greensboro would be only a few minutes away. "They could have met anywhere along the line, but Cal never reached the fame that O. Henry did, so there isn't as much available about the man."

"Couldn't the dedication be some other Cal Baxter?"

"Of course. Except how many Cal Baxters were there living close to Greensboro, North Carolina at the right age and time to have known O. Henry. Even if they met in Honduras, they'd have that commonality to befriend each other over. Plus, O. Henry died in 1910 and Cal Baxter inherits all this money in 1912. Doesn't that seem a little odd?"

"That's two years apart. Anybody could have died in that time and given money to Cal. I think you might be stretching, hon."

"That's because I can feel there's a connection here, I just can't find it, yet."

Reading Max perfectly, Sandra asked, "What can we do to help?"

"First, send Drummond to join me. I don't want to be checking out a dead man's house by myself. Not with all that's going on. Then I want you to check deeper into O. Henry, and particularly his aliases. There's a connection here, I promise, and maybe a fresh set of eyes will find it."

"You got it."

Before she could hang up, Max said, "Oh, and hon."

"Hmm?"

"I love you."

He could hear her smile. "Right back at you," she said.

Max laughed as he got off the highway and started checking street signs for Madison Drive.

Chapter 13

BY THE TIME DRUMMOND ARRIVED, Max had already found the place. It sat in the middle of a suburban street complete with house upon house, cars in the driveways, numerous old trees clinging to the last of Autumn's leaves. It was a great location for a family. Plenty of schools nearby. Access to the highway. Not too far from downtown. And Friendly Shopping Center only a few blocks north — a massive series of strip malls selling most everything a household might need.

"Why the heck would Freeman want to live here?" Drummond asked.

Max kept the answer to himself — Drummond wouldn't understand. Until recently, this was exactly where Max and Sandra had wanted to live. Not this specific street or city, but this life — the two-story home with a neat yard and a driveway. The neighborhood filled with the hope of children going off to school, playing in the street during the summers, ringing the doorbell on Halloween, and offering to shovel out cars in the winter. Freeman wanted to live here for the same reason Max and Sandra wanted to live here — for the promise of the future, for the blind faith that someday soon they could build that Norman Rockwell world around them, instead of being plagued with the Hulls and all their warped machinations.

Drummond stepped through the walls and Max heard the front door click open. He entered the house — empty. No furniture in the rooms, no paintings on the walls. Max checked the light switch and a ceiling mounted dome lit up.

"Electricity's still on," he said. No heat, though.

Max walked further in, his footsteps sounding hollow. He peeked out the front bay window. No *For Sale* sign in the yard.

"Doesn't look like anybody knew he was planning on leaving."

Drummond tipped his hat back as he looked around. "He wasn't leaving. Not yet. Remember now, he's jumped addresses several times. Guy like that doesn't settle into a place. This location was probably to keep up appearances that he was a normal fellow. He didn't want anybody bothering him, and if Hull looked into him — which would have been done before hiring anybody to take care of Baxter House — then having recently purchased this home would look good and stable."

They walked deeper into the house. The kitchen cupboards had plenty of instant soup while the freezer had been stocked with microwaveable dinners. Two used coffee mugs waited in the sink.

Upstairs Max found Sebastian's bedroom — the only room with anything in it. A mattress on the floor, a small television sitting on a milk crate, and stacks of books. It looked like the apartment of a college student.

"Over here," Drummond said, leaning near one stack of books.

Max saw the title *Cabbages and Kings* by O. Henry. Also in the stack, he saw *The Gift of the Magi and Other Stories* as well as a biography of O. Henry. "Guess we're not the only ones thinking there's a bigger connection to be found."

Next to the mattress, Max caught sight of a manila envelope. He swallowed back hard. A moment passed in which he expected to see the handwriting of Mr. Modesto on the outside and orders from the Hulls on the inside.

Instead, Max found photographs — lots of photographs. All different sizes, all black and white, many labeled on the back. Photos of Baxter House, streets of Winston-Salem, streets of Greensboro, an old locomotive roundhouse, the covered bridge leading into Old Salem, and more.

Drummond whistled. "You think he took all those?"

"No," Max said, flipping a few over. "Some of these are dated from the 1930s."

One photo depicted a small brick building surrounded by

open fields. On the back, somebody had written — *NGFS, Upper, before.* Max showed it to Drummond but the ghost only shrugged. Another photo showed a railroad bridge and on the back Max found the description — *Trollinger's bridge over Haw River.*

"What is all this?" he asked.

Drummond startled and he opened his coat pocket. He nodded at Leed, then shot out the door. Before Max had time to question him, Drummond returned. "We got trouble. Detective Rolson's here."

Max wondered how Leed knew about Rolson — assuming that's what the ghost blob said to Drummond — but that would have to wait for another time. Max gathered up the photos, stuck them in the envelope, and shoved the envelope down the back of his pants. He made sure his coat covered the envelope.

"You planning on talking with him?" Drummond asked, his incredulous tone unmistakable. "You do that, you'll end up in jail."

"I'm planning on hiding. I just don't want him knowing I've got the photos if he sees me."

"Well, he's going to see you if you don't move your ass."

As Rolson opened the front door, Max darted across the hall and into the opposite bedroom. There was only one place to hide — the closet. It had slats in the door, so as Max closed himself in, he could peek through the slats and see a bit of Sebastian's bedroom.

Drummond stood in front of the door and shook his head. "The closet? Really? Why didn't you go out the window or up into the attic? You make one little noise and Rolson will find you here with ease."

Though he wanted to argue, Max knew Drummond's last statement was right. He had to stay quiet or else Rolson would find him, in which case Drummond's initial statement would prove to be true — Max would end up in jail.

Rolson climbed the stairs in slow, plodding steps. Max pictured the tubby man laboring his way up, perspiring under a single-color sweater and a blazer. Though not necessary, Rolson clicked on a small penlight and inspected Sebastian's bedroom.

Drummond glided back toward Max. "You know, I have to hand it to this guy. If he were on the right track thinking you were the killer, he'd be doing a good job being a bug up your rear. He's been working out what moves you might make — going back to Baxter House, coming out here — and then making sure he's in those places to piss you off." Max scowled. "Don't get me wrong. I'm not saying I'm happy about this guy, but he's doing a good job."

Rolson turned his attention to the room across from Sebastian's — the same room in which Max hid. He played his penlight around the floor, never once bothering with the closet. Stepping near one of the room's two small windows, he rolled back and forth on his feet until he smacked his lips as if confirming this action tasted right to him. Without pause, he knelt and pulled a switchblade from his pocket. In seconds, he removed one of the floorboards.

"Damn," Drummond said. "This guy's the kind of cop I hate. You watching this, Max?"

Max watched. From inside his coat, Rolson removed an envelope filled with cash. He placed the envelope under the floor. Then he opened the plastic evidence bag and removed a few fibers which he let drift to the floor like falling leaves.

"He's setting you up. He can't solve the case on his own and you embarrassed him the other night at Baxter House, so he's bent on making you the killer. What really gets me is that guys like this convince themselves they're doing the right thing."

Rolson replaced the floorboard and headed downstairs. Drummond shoved his head through the closet. Max started but managed to keep his mouth shut.

"Look, you've got to move fast. Once he's gone, you have to get rid of that money and those fibers. He may not wait very long before pretending to come back here and find this bullcrap evidence. And wear gloves when you do it. You get your fingerprints on that envelope, and you're sunk."

The moment Max heard the front door close, he did as instructed. Putting on his winter gloves, he pulled up the floorboard, removed the envelope, swept the fibers in with the money, and closed the floorboard. As he descended the stairs, he heard Rolson's car back out of the drive.

"Tell me when he's gone," Max said.

"Count to ten or something. I've got to go with him. You toss that envelope and catch up with us. We've got to find out where he's going next." Drummond flew out of the house to follow Rolson.

"Wait." Max stood alone on the stairs. His head swirled and he found it difficult to breathe. Closing his eyes, he tried to slow his rapid pulse. He counted to ten.

When he opened his eyes, he saw nothing, heard nothing — Rolson had left. Max rushed out of the house toward his car. Halfway across the street he remembered the envelope in his hand and walked fast toward the neighbors trash can. He wanted to run but feared he might cause somebody in a nearby house to look out a window.

At the trash can, he paused. Glancing in the envelope, he only saw hundred dollar bills. There had to be at least two thousand dollars. If he took the money, he and Sandra could pay off a lot of bills and still have enough to keep the heaters running through the winter.

"Don't be an idiot," he muttered.

If he got caught with that cash on him, he would be helping Rolson frame him. Even if he didn't get caught, a sudden increase in his measly bank account would be evidence as well. It hurt, but Max let the envelope fall into the trash can. He stared at it. Even considered reaching in for it. But finally, he let the can close and returned to his car.

Pulling onto the road, Max felt a drag line connecting him back to that money. It tugged at him, stretching him, but he drove on.

Drummond swooped in. "Get on Business 40 West." Then he swooped out.

Five minutes later, Drummond returned. "Take the

Kernersville exit." And he was gone.

Max followed Drummond's directions. He drove right by Korner's Folly and his body shuddered. He could feel the ghosts residing in the attic of that strange house looking at him. *We almost had you here with us,* they would be saying. It seemed ages ago that he had been sneaking around that place, and now, it was no more than an old house he drove by.

Fifteen minutes passed before Drummond returned and settled on the passenger seat. "Don't go too fast. There's a turn coming up. Then you go about five miles and there's an abandoned gas station on the right. We can park a bit back on the left and get a good view of what's going on there."

"Which is what?"

"Looks like Rolson has the same addiction as Luther Boer — up ahead, it's another Midnight Fight."

Chapter 14

MAX SPIED ON THE RUNDOWN GAS STATION from far up the road. He watched through binoculars he had bought months earlier at Drummond's insistence. Thankfully, Drummond had not rubbed it in his face.

"Aren't you glad I made you buy those?" Drummond said.

At least, he hadn't rubbed it in right away.

From a rental truck, three men worked hard unloading boxes, folding chairs, tables, a generator, and all the other necessities required to convert the station into an illegal boxing arena. Rolson had parked next to the rental truck. A fourth man, tall and dressed in a fine suit, stepped out from the gas station and approached Rolson. They shook hands, exchanged a few words, and then the tall man ushered Rolson inside.

"Rolson keeps getting dirtier and dirtier," Drummond said. "Makes me sad."

"Am I seeing this right? Rolson's getting paid to look the other way on this boxing thing and maybe to make sure no other cops take notice. That's why he was the one in charge of me when I got beat up at the fight in Winston-Salem."

"Looks that way. Otherwise, how would he know this place was out here?"

Max continued to watch through the binoculars though nothing had changed. "You think he works for Hull, too? That witch I saw connects the boxing with the Hulls."

"I doubt it. You know what Hull's like. He wouldn't be messing with a loose gun like Rolson — planting fake evidence, framing you — it's all rather sloppy for a Hull endeavor."

"Still. If he's not with Hull, this is an awfully big coincidence."

Drummond snickered. "Let me put it a different way. I don't think Rolson knows he's working for the Hulls, though he probably is working for them. If they really do run this boxing thing, then it's their money bribing him. Now that I think about it, I wouldn't be surprised if they had set up the whole Midnight Fights to lure in gamblers, get them on the hook for a large sum, and use those debts to their advantage. Any big, illegal organization needs leverage against cops to force them into the fold. Despite what it seems like in the media, most cops are hard-working, decent folk. Just not enough corrupt ones out there to use. So, they set 'em up through gambling debts. That's probably how they got Luther Boer."

Rolson stepped out of the building with the old witch at his side. His eyes searched around as if expecting a gang of bandits to attack at any time. When they reached the car, he held the door open for the witch before walking around to the driver's side.

Drummond sighed. "On second thought — ain't no way he's escorting a witch and doesn't know who his dealing with."

Rolson's car backed into the street and turned to face Max. As the car approached, Max scooted low in his seat. Drummond spun around and watched.

"He's gone. You can get up."

"We should follow him, right?"

"Absolutely. We've got to know where that witch is going."

As Max started the car, his cell phone rang. He checked the call — Cecily Hull. He turned the car off. Showing the caller ID to Drummond, Max took a deep breath and gathered his thoughts.

When ready, he answered. "Hello."

"Hello, Mr. Porter. It's been a few days, and I thought that should be ample time for you to have fully considered my offer."

"I thought my wife made our opinion fairly clear."

He swore he could hear her titter — a horrid sound. "Do you really think posturing like that would dissuade me? I'd have never accomplished anything, if that were true. No, Mr. Porter, I've been waiting and watching."

"Watching?"

"Of course. I have my own people who specialize in keeping tabs on those I'm interested in. It seems to me that you are getting close to some big answers."

Max glanced in the rear view mirror — no sign of Rolson. "That's funny because I haven't a clue what the questions are. Let me ask you something though. Detective Rolson — is he on the Hull payroll? How many of the police are working for you?"

"Good going," Drummond said. "Press her and she might slip up, give us something useful."

Cecily sniffled as if dealing with Max's pedestrian questions had fouled her air. "Police? Oh, I don't know. As a lowly woman in this absurdly patriarchal family, I'm not privy to that information. However, you can rest assured that this isn't the world of Serpico. In Winston-Salem, we may have a few police officers or detectives or what-have-you who value us and are willing to aid us in our needs, but we don't go around bribing those in authority. We have no interest. After all, we have far more powerful tools at our disposal."

"You mean witchcraft."

"Amongst other things."

Drummond leaned closer to listen. "She's dodging. Don't let up, now."

Max shooed him off. "What else do you have besides witchcraft?"

"Money, of course."

"Obviously. What I mean is —"

"Mr. Porter, that's enough. You are, and have always been, a mere pawn to us. There have been times when you've been a powerful pawn, but now is not one of those times. If you wish to understand what your real role in all that's going on is, then you'll have to agree to work for me. Otherwise, I see no value in our conversation."

"I'm sorry to hear that because there's no way Sandra and I

will ever work for a Hull again."

"Then I'm afraid you're going to have a very bad day tomorrow."

Before Max could find out what that threat meant, Cecily ended the call. Max had to laugh, though. Lately, every day had been a very bad day for him.

With a frustrated huff, Drummond lowered his hat over his eyes. "C'mon. Let's go home."

Max bit back the sarcastic comments in his head. They had lost Rolson and the witch, and they had pulled little more than a threat from Cecily. He had to agree with Drummond's frustration.

Closing his eyes, Max exhaled. Time to drive home. He opened his eyes and checked the rear view mirror. The horned-beast stared back at him.

"Shit," Max yelled, wrenching his body around to see the backseat.

Empty.

"What is it?" Drummond looked all around, ready for action.

"I ... I ... Is there a ghost in the backseat?"

"I don't see any ghosts anywhere. The area's empty. You saw another ghost?"

Slouching back in his seat, Max shook his head. "I don't know what I saw." He reached down to put the car in Drive when he noticed his fingers tingled — the same fingers that had touched the circle painted on Cal Baxter's floor.

That can't be good, he thought and drove off, letting the hypnotism of the road ease his mind.

Chapter 15

"WAKE UP," SANDRA SAID, shaking Max's shoulder. "Money day."

Max lifted his head only to have gray sweatpants and a black t-shirt thrown in his face. "Good morning to you, too," he said and quickly dressed.

In order to stay financially afloat, Sandra and Max had decided to strictly limit their spending. Once a week, they walked up to the bank at Oliver's Crossing, a strip mall situated a short distance north of them, and withdrew all the cash they needed for the next seven days. If they had anything left at the end of the week, they usually saved it. This week, however, they decided to splurge on some frozen yogurt at the TCBY next to the bank. Sandra liked cold treats in the winter, and Max liked making Sandra smile.

As they trudged up the road, passing the gas station and then the fire department, Sandra leaned against Max for warmth. The crisp morning air lay still against their skin — thankfully, the harsh winds that often blew throughout the winter had taken the morning off. Sandra started going over the case, discussing each bit they had learned, trying to see how it all fit together, and Max joined in.

"You know what really bothers me about all this?" he said.

"Besides murder, witchcraft, and the Hulls?"

"Yeah, besides those things. The part that keeps bugging me is why did Sebastian hire us in the first place? What could we have found that he couldn't get on his own?"

"We found the hidden room in Baxter House."

Cars whisked by as Oliver's Crossing neared. Max held Sandra closer. "Given enough time, I think he would've found that room on his own. And for all we know, he actually did find it — or at the least, he was closing in on it. I think that's what got him killed."

"Except we don't know for sure why he was murdered. We only think there's a connection to that room, the House, and that those two things connect to Hull."

"I'm sick of hearing that name. I swear, when we're done with this case, I hope we never have to deal with them again."

They walked into the bank, filled out a withdrawal slip, and handed it to Ms. Birch, the teller. "Good morning, Mr. and Mrs. Porter," Ms. Birch said. She knew every customer by name and that local touch always thrilled Max. It gave him a sense that communities still existed even as people stretched their worlds further and further apart.

As Ms. Birch clacked away at her keyboard, wrote something down, and clacked some more, Max noticed the stern worry on her face. "Something wrong?" he asked.

She trembled out a smile. "N-No. The computer's just giving me a little problem. Hold on a moment, please." She walked from behind the counter, across the lobby, and entered a manager's office.

"What's that all about?" Sandra asked.

When Ms. Birch returned, she had Ms. Arnez following along. The tapping of their heels on the floor sounded like nails pounding into a wall. *No,* Max thought, *pounding into our coffin.*

Ms. Arnez stopped in front of them. "I apologize for the inconvenience, but apparently there's been a hold put on your account. I can't authorize any withdrawals until the hold is removed."

"A hold?" Sandra's voice rose. "You mean our account is frozen?"

"That's right. I suggest you contact a lawyer and check with either the police or the D.A.'s office to find out why this has happened, if you don't already know."

"Does it look like we know?"

Shifting on her feet, Ms. Arnez said, "Please, calm down. I know this is disconcerting, but since you didn't know this was being done, it's most likely a simple mistake. It's happened before. The D.A. wants to freeze assets of somebody whose name is close to yours. Porter isn't that uncommon a name, after all. I'm sure you can get it cleared up quit quickly."

"What are we supposed to do for money until then?"

"Normally, I'd offer to loan you some emergency funds for the short term, but I'm sorry. We can't help you. When accounts are frozen due to legal actions, my hands are tied. But I promise you, the moment you clear this up, we'll be happy to get you cash right away."

With an uncomfortable smile and a nod, Ms. Arnez walked back to her office.

Max thrust his hands in his coat pockets and led the way outside. "Looks like we're skipping TCBY today. We need to hold on to that extra cash."

They headed back to their trailer. Though Max still held Sandra close, the cold air chilled him under his skin. He knew the Hulls were powerful, of course — he understood they had hands in the police and politics and magic — but the idea that they could freeze his assets disturbed his sense of how the world worked. Public corruption was one thing, but manipulating a person's private life burrowed deep into him and left him questioning whether or not they could stand up to the Hulls anymore.

But another thought struck him, and he laughed. To answer Sandra's curious look, he said, "In order for us to cause this kind of reaction, we must be getting close to the truth — especially about Sebastian's murder."

"Doesn't feel like much of a *Go Team* moment."

"Being close to victory and achieving victory are two different things. But we're close."

Sandra wrapped her arms around Max's waist. "I hope you're right because being close to victory feels a lot like being close to defeat."

"Oh, honey, that doesn't sound like you. You're usually the one telling me we've got to push forward, suffer through it, and it'll all work out one way or the other."

"Having our money cut off changes things. How are we going to fight back when we can't even afford a loaf of bread? Or gas — how are we going to get around this place if we can't afford to drive our cars?"

Max held the trailer door open for Sandra. "Isn't that what our cookie jar is for?"

Sandra stepped over to the refrigerator and pulled down the cookie jar from above. She removed a layer of cookies and turned the jar over on the small dinette. Change rattled out and with a few shakes, she dumped the cash out as well. They counted it up in desperate silence.

At length, Sandra sat back. "Not bad. We can get by a few more days on that. A week if we stretch it."

"Then we stretch it." He scooped the money back into the cookie jar. "So, where do we begin?"

Drummond cleared his throat. "You could try back here."

"Get out of our bedroom," Max said.

"It's not really a bedroom. More like a bedspace."

"Then get out of our bedspace. What were you doing in there? Wait. Don't answer that."

Sandra smirked. "Do I need to burn the sheets now?"

"Relax, you two." Drummond drifted towards them. "I was looking over those photos we nabbed at Freeman's house. If we're going to figure out what he was after, what the Hulls are hiding that he may have found, then it makes sense to retrace his steps."

"Good idea," Max said.

"It's a pretty standard move. You should pay more attention. I've been doing this a long time. You'll learn a few things." Drummond waved his hand to stop Max from throwing out a sarcastic response. "Look, I'll make this simple enough for you. These pictures are all over the area, but several of them involved the railroad. So, that seems the most promising place to start."

Max walked over to the bed and brought back the photos. Five of them were of the same place — a large roundhouse filled with old locomotives and a few diesel engines. "If we're going by the logic of what Sebastian had the most pictures of, then this is the place to start."

"Hey, you are learning."

"Only problem is we have no idea where this building is."

Drummond rolled his shoulders which made him look larger. "*You* have no idea where the building is. Me, on the other hand, *I* know exactly where it is."

"You're going to make me guess?"

"We don't have time for that kind of fun. This is the North Carolina Transportation Museum."

"Never heard of it."

"It's in Spencer. Small town about a half-hour from here."

Sandra dug her hand in the cookie jar and pulled out forty dollars. She stared at the cash for a moment, and Max felt the same desire he read on her face — shove the money back in the jar, forget everything, close their eyes, and wish it all away. But their eyes met, and they both knew the only way to deal with the Hulls — push forward.

Max smiled. "Let's get some gas and hit the road."

Sandra handed him the money and grabbed the car keys.

Chapter 16

MAX ACCELERATED ONTO ROUTE 85 SOUTH toward Spencer. The steady white noise of wheels on the pavement weaved around the tense silence in the car. With no access to money, Max guessed Sandra thought the same things he did — every mile in the car meant cash out of their pocket, every exerted muscle that needed food meant cash out of their pocket, every moment of life meant cash out of their pocket.

On the backseat in a bag next to Drummond sat the lunch Sandra had prepared — two peanut butter and jelly sandwiches, tap water in a thermos. Max's stomach groaned at the mere thought of the meager fare. It seemed crazy that they had to spend more on gasoline to feed the car than they could on the food to feed themselves.

"No, no, no, I've got to stay with them," Drummond said.

Max glanced back to see Drummond talking to his pocket once again. "What's Leed want?"

With a perturbed grimace, Drummond said, "He's being a pain because he wants to help and he doesn't have a body in which to do it. So, he's asking for me to be his body."

"You can do that? Let him possess you or something?"

"No, no. Nothing like that. He wants me to leave you all and go to the library with him." Drummond said the word *library* as if it had caused a little vomit to rush up his throat. "He wants to do research on the witch, curses, stuff like that. I admit it was his area of expertise and he might be able to help us out, but you guys need me."

Sandra snorted. "I think we'll be fine on our own. We're going to a railroad museum. Unless you once dated an engineer who later became a witch."

"Oh, very funny. I'll have you know I dated plenty of women who never turned to magic, witchcraft, or anything arcane."

Max knew Drummond hated the library. He also knew that Leed would be a good researcher. It would drive Drummond crazy being forced to look up books, turn pages, and do all the labor of research so that Leed could read the texts, but the idea of having expert help hard at work while Max and Sandra did the on-site research appealed to Max. He thought it might also give Leed a sense of purpose.

"It's a good idea. Drummond, go ahead and help Leed. We'll be fine with this on our own. See if you two can turn up something."

"Sure," Drummond said, the scowl on his face and the growl in his throat not nearly as accommodating. To his pocket, he said, "Enough already, you're getting your way. I'm going, I'm going." Seconds later, Drummond disappeared.

At first, neither Max nor Sandra spoke. Less than a minute later, however, they both broke into hysterical laughter. The wonderful release warmed Max.

"Is it wrong that I found that so fun?"

Through rapid giggles, Sandra managed, "Not at all, Honey, not at all."

Shortly after, they exited the highway and found the entrance to the museum — a road nestled between two grassy mounds with an unlit sign easily missed. Though the small town of Spencer designated the area with homes and a few local businesses, the majority of the land remained for the museum. As Max drove up to the grass and gravel parking area, he understood why.

The "museum" was not a specific building but rather an enormous acreage that had once been an active rail yard with numerous spurs to handle a huge volume of rail traffic. All of Spencer had existed to service the yard. But those days were long gone. Most of the rail spurs had been removed, and all that remained were a few nonstop rail lines, several old buildings (now converted into museum walk-throughs), and the shining jewel of the museum — the roundhouse.

Max got out of the car and took one look at the depot ahead. They were supposed to go in there to pay for tickets, but the idea of giving up more cash twisted his gut hard.

Reading his mind, Sandra said, "Let's skip that part. Chances are that whatever we're looking for isn't part of the routine tour."

"Yeah. Doesn't look like they mind if you walk around. Probably won't be able to get in the buildings though."

"I hate to say it, but a ghost would be handy right now."

"Let's walk. See what we see. If we decide we need to get in any of the buildings, we can either come back here and pay up or send Drummond back later. Unless you happen to see any other ghosts around. They might help."

Sandra turned her head as she checked out the area. "Looks like we might have a few back there. Probably old railworkers killed on the line. No telling if they'll be friendly or not."

Offering his arm, Max said, "We don't need to worry over that now. Let's go for a walk."

They crossed a wide, grassy area with concrete pathways cut in. Max imagined that in the spring and summer this would be a lovely place to come for a picnic or an afternoon stroll. It was a park for the train lovers. With winter pushing in, however, few people came, and those that did hurried their bundled bodies towards the various buildings.

As they passed between two massive structures — long ago used to house machine shops, warehousing, and construction of all sorts — Max felt dwarfed by the sheer power of the trains. A track ran down the middle of the street and snaked off toward the roundhouse ahead. A steam locomotive sat on the track, waiting for an engineer to guide it somewhere.

Of course, Max had seen plenty of large, man-made structures — skyscrapers, jumbo jets, cruise ships, and such. Something about this locomotive, though, impressed him more. It wasn't simply the thing's size. No, it was the power inside it. Max could feel the explosive force within this massive hunk of metal straining to be free.

"I know how you feel," he whispered, and an image of the horned beast flashed in his mind.

Before he could ponder what that meant, Sandra kissed his cheek.

"What was that for?" he asked.

"Do I need a reason?"

He looked at her and leaned in to give her a more passionate kiss. But she put her hand on his chest and pushed back.

With a cute wink, she said, "It was just an 'I love you' peck. We've still got work to do here." She pecked his other cheek and they headed on.

The roundhouse took up a large swath of land. With thirty-seven bays housing forty locomotives, it remained one of the largest preserved roundhouses in the country. Each bay of the crescent-shaped building had a track flush with the pavement that shot straight toward the fully-operational turntable — one of the last in existence.

A turntable was a large piece of track bridging a circular pit that could turn a full rotation. Thus, a locomotive could drive onto the track, stop, and be turned around. In the case of the roundhouse, it saved the trouble of having to design thirty-seven complex switches. Instead they have one turntable track that could service each bay of the roundhouse.

While Max found the whole setup ingenious, and part of him wanted to come back under less stressful circumstances so he could look in depth as to how it all worked, he had a job to do. The turntable had his attention because of the deep pit. That could be an excellent place to hide something.

Except they weren't even sure if what they sought was hidden. He didn't recall Sebastian having a photograph of the turntable — just the roundhouse. Did that mean the turntable was not important? Or that Sebastian had made a mistake in discounting its value?

"I wish I knew what we were looking for," he said.

Sandra blew on her hands. "That would make it easier. Especially in this cold."

Max pointed to a door on the closest side of the

roundhouse. "Let's go inside there. Even if they stop us from going further, we can at least warm up a little."

They entered a gray lobby, more like a wide hallway, with blown-up black and white photos on the walls. The photos depicted the hard work of railroad men — covered in soot, shoveling coal, reaching into these ferocious machines, praying not to lose an arm while trying to tighten a hard to reach bolt. Further along the hall, large windows allowed a clear view of the first few bays, each holding an old steam locomotive.

Max stopped to look closer. Craning his neck, he could see clearly through gaps in the track. Underneath was another level — one for repairmen to have access to the bellies of the engines. It reminded him of how auto mechanics used to work before they invented the hydraulic lifts found in most garages today. Back then, they had a trench dug into the ground. A car would be driven over it and the mechanic would be in the trench. Same concept here except the grander scale of the roundhouse required a grander trench — an entire sub-floor spanning the entire roundhouse and possibly more.

At the far end of the lobby, an elderly man sat next to a small podium and a glass door. "Y'all have tickets?" he asked.

Sandra smiled over at him. "How much are they?"

The man pointed to a clearly marked sign. "Six dollars for an adult gets you in all the buildings on the premises."

Max gestured to the sub-floor. "Do we get to go down there?"

"No, sir," the old man said.

Max looked through the window again. To Sandra, he said, "I doubt the answer's in a regular tour. If it were that easy to find, this would have been all over long ago." He turned back to the old man. "Is there a different tour that goes down there?"

The old man's lips rose in a devilish grin. "No, sir. That's for the volunteers."

"Volunteers?"

"Yup. All the people down there working on the restorations and maintenance of these wonderful engines, they are all volunteers. Do it for the love of railroading."

"What if we were thinking about volunteering and we wanted to check it out down there?"

"Well, then, I'd be happy to show you around. But I think we both know you aren't really interested in volunteering."

The old man remained at the podium, that creepy smile on his lips. He didn't get angry, didn't ask them to leave, but he wasn't helping them either.

Sandra cleared up the matter. "You'll have to excuse my husband. He can be a dolt sometimes. Perhaps a private donation would get a few minutes downstairs?"

"Of course, ma'am. We're always happy to entertain the rail enthusiasts with special treatment."

Sandra placed a twenty dollar bill in his hand. When he didn't budge, she placed another. After the third, he hesitated, but the stern look on her face — one Max knew too well — warned the old man off trying for more.

"Follow me," he said and led them through a side door.

As they walked behind him, Max leaned close to Sandra and whispered, "You're right. I can be a bit of a dolt sometimes."

At the bottom of a metal staircase, the old man opened a door. "Here you go. And if you cause any trouble, you snuck down here while I was off pissing. Got it?"

"Thank you," Sandra said.

After the old man left, they walked along the back wall. The entire floor resembled a mechanic's garage. Tools of all sizes and shapes lay about. A radio played Led Zeppelin. Calendars stuck to the walls and tool chests — though instead of nude women, most of these depicted long trains cutting through mountain passes.

Several men and women meandered about — some working, others chatting. They noticed Max and Sandra but none seemed bothered by the intrusion. None of them seemed particularly welcoming either. Max had no idea where to begin until he noticed the young man working under one of the locomotives.

He had his dark hair buzzed close to this head and despite

the cold, he wore only an oil-stained t-shirt and jeans. He hung a lamp near where he intended to work and stretched to reach something in the locomotive above. When he did this, Max noticed a tattoo on his forearm — a circle with a swirling yin-yang design. Just like the one he saw on the witch's hand at the fights.

"That's our man," Max said, and waved until he got the young mechanic's attention.

"You people lost?" the man said as he walked over.

Max put out his hand. "We're looking to talk to somebody."

The young man shook Max's hand. "You're in luck. I'm somebody. Name's Pete Venter. You?"

"Max Porter. This is my wife, Sandra."

Pete took Sandra's hand gently and gave it a graceful kiss. "So, what is it you want to talk about?"

"I'm not sure," Max said. He hadn't thought this far through and now his mind blanked.

Once more, Sandra rescued him. "We're gathering strange stories for a book on the weirder side of railroads."

"The weirder side?"

"You know, like haunted railcars and mysterious happenings. A place as old as this has got to have some cool history to it, and we're looking for the history that doesn't make it into the usual books."

Pete scratched his chest with a blush. "I don't know about hauntings or anything mysterious. I mean we just work on the engines here. You ought to talk with some of the old dudes. They probably know all kinds of stories."

Max gave Pete a playful bump on the shoulder. "Aw, c'mon. You look like a popular guy around here. I'm sure you know a good story that the others wouldn't dare share."

"Well, I know one story, but it ain't got ghosts or anything like that. I'm not sure it's what you're looking for."

"Try us."

Pete glanced back at the other volunteers who appeared to be embroiled in a deep discussion of HO-scale versus O-scale for model railroading. "The story I know is about lost gold.

You think that might be of interest?"

"Definitely," Max and Sandra said simultaneously.

"Okay, then, here it is — a long time back there was a town called Company Shops. It's now part of Burlington, but back then it was basically a place to repair trains as they passed through the state. At the tail end of the Civil War, a shipment containing bales of cotton and kegs of gold was sent to Company Shops. Only problem was nobody had ordered it, and there was no designated person or company to deliver it to. It just got sent. The locals in the area swiped all the cotton but the gold — well, no one knows what happened to it. It vanished. Lot of people still look for it. You go out to Burlington and check the line, old Trollinger's bridge, anywhere related to the route that train would've traveled, you'll find people looking for the gold. Some come all the way from California with their metal detectors. It's ridiculous."

Max said, "Because you don't think it's true?"

"Oh, it's true. It happened. But we're talking 1865. Nobody's going to find that money. It's probably long gone and already spent by now, anyway."

"Thanks, Pete. You've certainly given us a strange story."

"Not all that strange when you think about it. I mean, the war was lost. Things around here were descending into madness. The Northern soldiers were looting everywhere they went. It was a mess. Can't say I'm surprised that somebody tried to ship a bunch of gold out of here nor that it got intercepted."

"Guess you're right about that. But kegs of gold don't simply vanish. Not easily anyway. Even in 1865, trails of evidence can be found."

"Maybe so," Pete said. "Still, people been trying since it went missing. That's nearly a hundred and fifty years, and nobody's found squat."

They thanked Pete for his time and made their way back to the car. Driving toward Winston-Salem, Max tapped his fingers on the wheel and mumbled to himself.

"You going to let me in on your conversation?" Sandra

asked.

"Oh, sorry."

"Don't be sorry. Just tell me what you're thinking. Everyone's after this gold, right?"

"If it's real. When we get back, I want to go to the library and look into this. Stories of lost gold aren't the kind of thing that gets forgotten. Somebody will have written about it. But I'm feeling optimistic on this one."

"A gut feeling? I'll alert Drummond."

"While you're having fun ribbing me, make sure to call Cecily Hull and set up a meeting with her. I think we'll have a far more interesting conversation now."

Max focused on the road as his mind went over the details of their talk with Pete Venter. The gold story was only part of it, of course. That symbol tattooed on his arm — that had to be important. Max resolved to research that as well, but he had a strong suspicion he wouldn't like the answer.

Chapter 17

MAX NEEDED TO CLEAR HIS MIND before facing Cecily Hull later that evening, so he went to the one place that he knew would help — the library. Before he reached a table and removed his coat, Leon hurried to his side.

"I'm so glad you showed up. I was afraid I'd miss you when my shift ended."

Max loved the giddy enthusiasm of his friend. "I take it you found something about Sebastian."

"No. But that O. Henry story you found — I looked into Cal Baxter some more. In particular, I learned that his famous house has had an interesting history."

Leon launched into a tale that took Max by surprise. In addition to Baxter House's odd creation and eccentric owner, the place had a dark reputation. Over the decades since Cal Baxter's death and the Hull family's purchase of the house, four people had attempted to break into the building.

Leon found no record of what they sought. "Guess they figured anything worth building up in secret has got to be hiding something. Besides which, the whole thing was an unanswered mystery, and some people cannot let that kind of thing go."

With an excited shake, Leon showed Max several grainy copies of old newspaper articles. There was Samantha Shoemaker, a devout Christian woman, who wanted to free Cal Baxter from haunting the house. Another was Alex Crane, a young man who often got teased for wearing a leather bomber jacket though he had never served. In the 1980s, a young man from Japan traveled to check out the house. Ushiro Takashi looked amusing with his neck garnished in a mass of gold chains and his body proudly wearing a Mr. T sweatshirt. The last page showed Alan Peck — an older man wearing a heavy, dark coat and a hunter's cap.

"The weirdest part about all of this is the fates of these four people. All of them disappeared. They never came out of the house again. Police were summoned, but when they searched the house, they didn't find anything. Not even a hint that those people had gone in."

Max looked over the pictures again. "Thanks. I don't know how this fits in, but I'm glad for the extra info."

"I thought you might like it. Good luck with the rest of your search. I got to get home."

As Leon shuffled off, Max thought about the secret room. He never saw signs that people had been killed in there — assuming these unfortunate mystery-hunters were killed — but then Sebastian's murder had enough strangeness about it to suggest that these disappearances could have equally strange answers behind them. Perhaps Cal had built another secret room in the house.

He set the pictures aside and dived into more research on finding Lilla. An hour later, with little to show, he packed up and headed home. He didn't feel that much better, but Leon's contribution gave him a sense of progress.

That night, Sandra and Max met Cecily Hull at the Tokyo Steakhouse. Cecily offered to pay for dinner, so the Porter's thought it best to go for something moderately expensive. Plus, they both enjoyed Japanese cuisine and had not been able to afford it for a long time.

Tokyo Steakhouse was the kind of place where the chefs put on a show, cooking the food in front of the diners with plenty of fast-paced and flashy knife-work. Cecily purchased a private room, leaving clear instructions that the chef should simply cook the food and avoid the show. Though this disappointed Max, he considered that the food came free, so he would keep all whining to himself.

"What? No show?" Drummond, naturally, had no problem complaining. "Bad enough I can't eat any of this food, but I can't even get the show. What a cheat."

After the chef prepared their meals and left, Max and Sandra dug in. Cecily's look of disgust did nothing to prevent their ravenous attack on the shrimp, chicken, and rice. Five minutes later, Max patted his belly.

Cecily forced a smile. "Glad you enjoyed this. Now, I'm assuming we're meeting tonight so that we can discuss your working for me?"

"No," Max said, enjoying the shocked look on her face. "We're meeting so that I can tell you to back off — unfreeze our assets and leave us alone. If you don't, we'll find that gold before you or Tucker or any of the others looking for it. We'll find it first — you know that. That's why you want us to work for you. So, leave us be or we'll get the gold and you won't have anything to fund your fight against Tucker with."

Cecily stared at Max a moment before breaking into laughter. "Bless your heart, aren't you adorable, thinking you have something to threaten me with. But, you see, I don't want the gold."

Drummond drifted toward the door. "Hope you have a backup plan. If it helps, nobody's out here watching or anything. She's all alone."

Sandra pushed her empty plate aside. "Perhaps you can tell us what it is you do want. And don't give us your crap about us having to work for you. We know this gold is involved. We'll get the rest of the story eventually."

Cecily clicked her tongue. "For such a noteworthy researcher, I'm surprised you haven't learned everything you need to know already."

"I see," Max said. "You don't think we're that close. Well, let me share with you what you should already know. And if you don't know any of this, then consider it a warning as to how good I actually am. The gold goes missing in 1865. This is a pretty well-documented case — newspaper reports, rail yard reports, even a reference in some Union army reports. What isn't reported at all, because nobody could figure it out, was who the gold was meant to go to."

Drummond's head whipped toward them. "You don't mean — Hull?"

"There's only one family in all of North Carolina that I can think of who could pull off a carload of gold without any paperwork," Max said.

Cecily raised an eyebrow. "The Reynolds family could do it, too."

"Maybe. But they wouldn't. Your family, however — this is right up their alley. So, somebody with a lot of guts rips off your family's gold. I'm not sure what happened to this guy, but my guess is that the family employed a witch to curse the thief in an imaginative and tragic way. Unfortunately, for you, whatever spell you used did not result in a confession. So, the Hulls were out their gold."

"You can't prove any of this."

"This isn't a court of law. I'm merely pulling in the knowledge I have with the threads of information available to me — it's what I'm good at. I may not be exactly right, but I'm close. I can see it on your face."

"Don't think you're so smart. There's far more than you know." Cecily tried to look amused but Max could tell he had unnerved her.

"I have no doubt. In fact, I'm not sure what happened for the next twenty or thirty years — except that the Hulls couldn't find the gold. But I think I can guess what happened after that. See, in the 1890s, William Porter, better known as the writer O. Henry, was living down in Texas. He spent a lot of his time hanging out in hotel lobbies eavesdropping on all the rich people passing through. It was a great way to get news stories or ideas for fiction. I think one day he was doing his usual thing when he happened to overhear something about the Hulls missing gold."

"And how would that have happened if the man who stole the gold was silenced by a witch?"

"Nobody steals a trainload of gold by himself. He had an accomplice, maybe more than one. When O. Henry hears them talking, he knows exactly what it's about. After all, he's from

Greensboro. He would have been told stories about the gold while growing up. Whatever he heard that day, it clued him in to where to search for the gold. But he had his own problems to deal with, problems that required him to leave on the run for Honduras. By the time he returned and served his jail sentence, he had become a famous author and no longer required the gold."

"This is a very entertaining tale," Cecily said, but her tone fooled nobody.

"It gets better. See, even though O. Henry didn't need or want the gold, he wasn't going to let it go to waste. In 1909, as his life neared its end, he wrote a story and dedicated it to an old friend, Cal Baxter. I believe that story contains a hidden message for Cal that told him what O. Henry knew about the gold."

"Really, now, Mr. Porter. A secret message in a famous author's short story? I suppose you've cracked the code, too."

"Not at all. There's no point. We already know Cal figured it out and found the gold. Which is good news for all of us because the code wasn't easy. It took Cal three years and he knew O. Henry. How else to explain that massive yet mysterious inheritance he came into in 1912?"

"Perhaps a relative who died and left a fortune to Mr. Baxter."

With a derisive frown, Sandra said, "That would be the normal explanation. But the problem is that your family bought Baxter House the second it became available. Overpaid for it, too. In our line of work, we call that a coincidence. We don't like coincidence."

Drummond snorted in one gleeful burst. "Watch out, Max. I think your wife is getting a stronger taste for this."

Cecily ignored Sandra as she leaned closer to Max. "If I understand you correctly, you are saying the hidden gold is no longer hidden. That Cal Baxter found it, spent it on his mansion and his life, and it's all been absorbed into the banking system, investments, and such. Is that right?"

"Not in the least," Max said. "If all the gold had been

transferred into the system, there'd be nothing to search for. The gold would be gone and you would have no way to claim it. But the fact is that you and Tucker and Sebastian Freeman and probably others are still searching for it. Ergo, the gold is still around. Since nobody has found it, it's still hidden — just not hidden where it had been before."

Cecily's body tensed like a lioness ready to pounce. "Should I assume you know where the gold is then?"

"Why, Ms. Hull, didn't you ever learn not to assume?"

"Then you know nothing more than some history."

"I know that I've found out the full history in a short few days. And where the rest of you have had the same information for years and have been unable to find the gold, I've narrowed it down to a few key sites. That's why I know I'll get to it first. You know it, too — otherwise, we wouldn't be having this conversation. You want us to work for you so that you can get that gold."

Cecily sat back, a calm confidence taking over that worried Max. He had her on the edge and suddenly the whole thing shifted. What had he said wrong?

"Careful, Max," Drummond said. Max wanted to snap *I know, I know,* but he had to stay quiet.

Cecily tilted her head, forcing her hair to hang over one eye like a professional model. "You are so arrogant, so sure of what you know, that you don't listen very well. I do not want the gold. I'm a Hull. I have more money than I could possibly spend in a lifetime — money that neither Tucker nor Terrance nor any other Hull can touch. What I need is the chest that holds the gold. Give me that and you can keep the gold."

Max, Sandra, and Drummond stared at Cecily. Nobody spoke. Elsewhere in the restaurant, the clanking of chef's knives and the sizzling of meat formed a distant noise.

At length, Max said, "Did ... did you say we could keep the gold?"

"Oh, are you suddenly interested in what I have to say?"

"*Confused* might be a better word."

"Allow me to make it simple enough for you to understand.

I agree with your assessment of the history and the current situation. I agree that Cal Baxter did not convert all the gold into other assets. That gold was contained in special chests. I require those chests but not their contents. Therefore, my offer is this — come work for me, for this one case, and the pay will be any gold you find. I will take the chest. That's it."

Max looked to Sandra. Her expression read nothing but suspicion. To Cecily, he said, "There's something wrong here."

"There's a lot wrong here," Drummond said.

"If this was the deal you wanted to offer us, why not tell us that from the start? Why the bullying tactics, freezing our assets? Why not simply offer us the gold?"

Cecily placed her hands on the table. An insignificant gesture most of the time, but with her, it felt calculated and controlled — a way for her to maintain control over the pacing of the next part of the conversation. Max thought of the way a boxer could control the ring by stepping a certain direction, forcing the opponent to either follow or pay the consequences. He hoped his choices would not be so limited.

"First and foremost, I had nothing to do with the freezing of your assets. That was Tucker's doing. He doesn't want you around North Carolina and he is not pleased about your refusal to leave."

Sandra said, "That's all he's going to do? Make life uncomfortable for us?"

Max appreciated her bravado, but considering how greedily they had eaten their meal, he doubted Cecily bought into the idea that they were happily poor.

Cecily went on, "Tucker has had much to deal with to keep the peace in our family. This issue of Cal Baxter is but one problem among many. So, forgive him for not crushing you right away."

"He wouldn't do that anyway," Max said. "He likes to make people suffer. Isn't that right? Hulls are a vindictive bunch. They'd rather curse a man than kill him."

"Regardless, Tucker is the one that froze your assets. I tried to warn you and to leverage the event in my favor. As to the rest, I didn't offer the gold at first because I had hoped to avoid the offer. I'd much rather keep the gold, but when I saw your situation and when I realized the depth of your hatred toward my family, it seemed the only lure strong enough to entice you."

Drummond said, "I'm not buying this. Don't take this deal. You can't know how much gold is left, if anything. Some thief could have robbed the gold long ago and nobody knows it yet. You don't want to end up like Geraldo Rivera opening Capone's safe."

Before he could stop himself, Max said, "How do you know about Geraldo?"

"I'm dead. I'm not completely out of touch."

"Who's Geraldo?" Cecily's lost expression clamped Max's mouth.

"Nobody. Forget it. Just a reminder that we've been promised riches before, and look at us now. So, thank you for the dinner, but we'll not be working with you."

Cecily's fingers curled into fists. "In addition to the gold, I will add a daily stipend to ease your financial troubles until the case is over. How about one hundred dollars a day?"

Waving his hands frantically, Drummond said, "No! Don't do it!"

But Max and Sandra nodded. "You got a deal," Max said.

"Damn. What good is having a ghost around, if you won't listen to me? I'm going to wait in the car. You two can ruin your lives for a few dollars without me."

As Drummond left the room, Cecily brought out her credit card and tapped it on the table. A waiter whisked in and took the card.

"I recommend that you get started right away. While I'm hopeful that you will be as good as you claim in getting the chest of gold, I know Tucker is quite determined. Understand that if he gets control of the chest first, his wrath, the fierce power he has contained for now, will be unleashed. He won't play around with asset freezes. He'll abduct you both, torture you for years, then kill you and have his witch curse your remains. So get to work."

"No need for the threats. The gold is enough to get us working."

"Maybe, but you see, what happens to you is nothing compared to what he will do to me."

Max stood and put out his hand. "I understand. Don't worry. We'll find that gold."

Cecily's mouth turned upward with a Cheshire grin. "Welcome back to the family."

Chapter 18

DRUMMOND REFUSED TO SPEAK. However, he also refused to leave. Max and Sandra wanted to celebrate having cash in their pockets and the promise of a fortune in gold, but Drummond hovered in the back of the trailer glowering at them.

Finally, Sandra faced Drummond with a knife sharp glare. "We're not idiots. We know better than most what the Hulls are capable of. But for this one case, we can use them against themselves. Worst outcome is that we get the *per diem* for a week or so and then we're back to where we started."

"Are you crazy?" Drummond blurted. "Did you not listen to her? To what would happen if Tucker gets that gold? He'll raze you to the ground."

"All the more reason for us to accept Cecily's help. You don't really think Tucker would back off simply if we turned Cecily down? You know better."

Drummond crossed his arms and looked away. His sourness undercut their party but not enough to stop them. Max cracked open a ten-dollar bottle of champagne, and they drank every last drop before kicking Drummond out of their trailer so they could be alone.

When morning arrived, Drummond returned. "Tell me what I can do." Max noted the lack of enthusiasm in the ghost's voice, but at least he wanted to help.

"I've got something perfect for you," Max said. "Go find that witch from the fights. See if you can piss her off enough that she might let something slip. Sound fun?"

Drummond fought back at a smile. "I'm sure Leed would prefer more research, but we'll manage."

To Sandra, Max said, "Look into this photo for Trollinger

Bridge. And this other one marked NGFS — can you find out where that field is and what NGFS even means?"

"I'm on it," she said and snatched the photos.

"Good. I'm going back to Baxter House, see what we may have missed."

They all split off to their different tasks. As Max drove up toward the city, his fingers tapped the wheel with an involuntary shiver. After much thought the previous night, he had come to the conclusion that the creature he had been seeing came from having touched the circle at Baxter House. More importantly, he thought the creature must be an image sent from Cal Baxter.

The house had belonged to Cal and had been built in secret to Cal's specifications — which included the secret room. Drummond had been unable to locate Cal in the Other which suggested that Cal might still be in the house. These visions that kept coming to Max could very well be a message from Cal — and Max wanted to get a better connection.

He worried about what Sandra would say. In fact, he knew she would be furious when she found out — especially when she realized that he had sent her off looking into that bridge and NGFS not only because they needed the information, but mostly so that she wouldn't be around to stop his plan. He hated keeping her in the dark, but at least he hadn't lied. He simply omitted his full intentions.

When he reached Baxter House, he parked a block away again. The last thing he wanted was another pesky neighbor calling the police and alerting Detective Rolson. He walked around to the back of the house and went straight for the door Drummond had unlocked. Slipping inside with ease, he had to hand it to his old pal — that ghost knew a lot of useful tricks.

He moved fast, planning on barreling into the secret room and get to work, but when he entered the study, his legs stopped moving. He stood in front of the desk, facing the open wall, seeing the room beyond with its dark candle, cold walls, false doors, and painted circle. One thought repeated in his mind — *be careful.*

The last time he stood here, Rolson had attempted to arrest him. But all that time, Rolson never noticed the gaping hole in the wall or the secret room. How could he not see it? Could the room be protecting itself somehow?

Another thought entered Max's head — why hadn't Hull's people ripped this house to pieces? They owned the place. For the last bunch of days, they've been stuck because of the police, but before Sebastian's murder, they had free run of the place. With access to their personal witch, they could have easily found the secret room. Best Max could figure — either the Hulls had searched the house and determined the gold was not on the premises or the House employed some type of magic that prevented the Hulls from finding anything. There was clearly a ward preventing Drummond from entering the room, why not others?

It always came back to magic.

And that was why he came back, too.

"Make up your mind, Max," he said. "Either go in or get out." He had to assume that Rolson would find out he had broken in again, and that this time, he would be arrested without fail. Time was ticking away.

Max pulled out his phone and texted Sandra: *Hey, Hon. Find anything?*

A few seconds later, his phone chimed. *Nothing yet. Only just started. You?*

He typed back: *Nothing yet.* But that made the decision easy. They needed the case to move forward. Max puffed up his chest, and though his bowels gurgled, he entered the room with the painted circle.

Though the room had not changed from his previous visit, everything about it seemed different. The black candle looked darker. The walls looked colder. The paint looked thicker. Even the barren furnishings looked more barren.

Perhaps the change had resulted from his own anxiety, but Max doubted it. Magic behaved strangely, and he had become accustomed to its unpredictable nature — well, he had learned to live with it, even if accepting it proved more difficult.

Mostly, though, Max knew that he didn't know enough. If given the choice, he would rather deal with ghosts. That, at least, made sense.

"Great," Max muttered to the empty room. "Now I'm thinking ghosts make sense."

He walked around the circle, looking for any hint of what he should do. He had seen several magic circles before — mostly drawn by people trying to kill him — but the symbols had never been consistent. He guessed that the different combination of symbols produced different results. The symbols at his feet meant nothing to him, though. The majority, he had never seen.

"Cal?" His voice sounded hollow against the stone walls. He looked at the stern portrait on the wall and waved. "Cal Baxter. My name is Max Porter. I'm the one you keep trying to contact. I'm here in your house. Tell me how I can help."

Silence.

Max squatted next to the circle. He considered touching the paint again, even dangled his fingers over it, but pulled back. *I just don't know enough about magic.* Following a hunch when researching worked fine, but doing so outside of books, in the practical world, often led to undesirable consequences — death being chief among them.

He pulled out his phone and brought up Sandra's number. She would know the answer. "Or she'd yell at me, tell me to get out of here, and nothing would be accomplished but the start of an ugly fight." Except he had nobody else to call.

Call? He looked at his phone. He didn't have to call anybody. Instead, he did a quick search for websites dealing with magic — the real thing. Tapping from one site to the next, he rushed through them until he recognized one of the sites Sandra had used before.

Reading for a few minutes, he found a lot of basic information he already knew. Then he saw the links for Spells, Curses, and Circles. Circles led him to a long scrollable page filled with symbol after symbol after symbol.

He didn't see how the images had been organized, and part

of him thought they hadn't been organized at all, but at the bottom of the page, he found another link that led to an explanation of how the symbols could be used. Basically, one constructed a sentence around the circle. The key symbols had to be at the key compass positions while the less important symbols filled in the gaps. Materials used in making the circle were important, and what the spellcaster said while standing over the circle was equally important.

"That's it?" Max closed his phone in frustration. He knew that somewhere on the Internet, maybe even on that specific site, he would find a more detailed and useful explanation, but he lacked the time for such research.

He stared at the circle. It seemed to shimmer — as if it had become a warm pool inviting him in for a dip. Maybe it would work. If he stood in the center and called out for Cal, maybe they would connect. Merely touching the circle had started this; perhaps jumping in fully would complete it.

Max.

That had not been his own thought, yet it echoed in his head. It had a complex voice as if more than one person spoke. A gentle, feminine voice coupled with a harsh, graveled masculine voice.

Come to me.

"Cal?"

Reach down.

Max looked at his feet. Though he had no recollection of moving, he now stood in the center of the circle. His head lolled and he rocked as if he had been drinking for hours. Part of him screamed to get out of the circle, but that scream grew quieter every second until he heard nothing but a steady hum.

He bent down, his hands swaying over the circle like a bad orchestra conductor, and he squinted against the bright shimmering. It never stopped. Back and forth the light played on his eyes, and his body flowed with the rhythm.

Reach down.

The multi-voice spoke over the steady hum and it made sense. He should reach down. He should touch the circle.

So, he did.

With a painful jolt like a kick to the head, Max's brain ignited with images. He saw the horned-beast hovering a few feet away. As the voice had been more than one voice, the image of the beast comprised other images, too.

He saw a scrawny character, hunched over with a weasel smile, and at the same time, he saw an overweight fellow, full of pride at his wealth. He saw an anklet of a gold cross and a leather bomber jacket. A fuzzy image, out of focus, hung in the back of his sight — a red and black checkered pattern. Separate, these images meant nothing, but together they formed the horned-beast. Yet Max could only see the pieces by turning his head one direction or the other. If he looked straight on, he only saw the intimidating visage of the horned-beast — large, hairy, angry.

Another jolt struck him simultaneously in the head and the gut. Max doubled over, gripping his stomach. He strained for air that didn't burn while hearing a long wheeze from his lungs.

He looked up. The horned-beast had vanished. For a second, Max's head cleared. He put a foot firmly in front, ready to launch out of the circle. He knew he was in trouble. But he could do that. He could get clear of the circle. All he had to do was push off —

Images flashed rapidly in his head — each one a bolt of lightning, bright and painful. Gold. Stacks of gold bars. Trains rolling. A man in the tropics scribbling over a piece of paper. A woman carving a circle into the ground — a witch. A battlefield of the Civil War — blue and gray racing toward each other, shouting, firing weapons. Gold, again. The horned-beast.

Max clutched his aching skull. "I don't know what you want!" He yelled to hear his own voice above the unrelenting hum.

You!

The word vibrated in his bones. He fell to his knees, and his body arched backward. Locked in a steady stream of cramped muscles and fiery jolts, he found it impossible to focus on any one thought.

Even as he heard Sandra's warnings repeating in his mind, he saw the horned-beast floating before him. Flashes of gold and trains blended with images of Sebastian and magic circles. He felt like he sat in an electric chair at a multiplex playing all its films at once.

The horned-beast lifted a clawed hand and dug into Max's head. No blood, no sense of tearing skin, but he sure knew the creature peered inside. Max's right arm flailed backward, smacking the tall candlestick. The black candle banged onto the floor and rolled toward the wall. The horned-beast never paused or even noticed the disruption. It simply continued to dig in Max's brain.

But it wasn't ripping up his gray matter. Rather, it seemed to be plugging into Max's memories. Every time it moved, old memories popped up before Max's eyes.

He saw his eighth birthday party — a pool party with kids running around at the YMCA, cake in their hands, sugar highs glazing over everyone's eyes. He saw an afternoon in high school — a bully who had followed him home one day, cornered him behind a church, and pummeled Max in the belly before sauntering off with a mean snicker. He saw his wedding — Sandra radiating love and beauty with every wide smile.

His memories shifted to more recent times — Korner's Folly, the witch coven, the Hull family, and even the German POW work camps set up in Butner. Then he saw the detective that had changed his life.

"Drummond," Max whispered. Though he would never admit it, a tear dribbled down the side of his face as he recalled meeting Drummond for the first time and all the difficulties they went through in order to free him from his curse.

The pain disappeared. The horned-beast flew back. Its eyes stared at Max for a moment, and Max swore he saw a hopeful look in that creature's expression.

It nodded at him, and Max passed out.

Chapter 19

"HOW DARE YOU," SANDRA SAID, her face so tight it looked as if it might fold in on itself. "After all we have been through, after all we have seen and done, you want to go off on your own to do such a stupid, reckless thing — dealing with magic like that."

"I was trying to protect you from —"

"Stop trying to protect me."

"I'm your husband and I love you. Of course I'm going to try to protect you."

"That's an excuse. You knew I would be against you doing this. I'm sure Drummond would be against you doing this. You weren't trying to protect me as much as you wanted to avoid having me stop you."

Max had no more to say. After all, she was right.

When he had awoken, his body had been moved from the secret room back into the study. He had gasped for air as if bursting from the ocean after nearly drowning. It took him ten minutes before he had enough control over his body to phone Sandra for help. To her credit, she didn't question him. She merely drove over and picked him up. But now that they had been home for an hour, now that they were safe, she wanted answers.

Unfortunately, caught up in her rage of the situation and his defense, neither of them gained any ground in finding answers — until Drummond entered the trailer and said, "I don't mean to pry but I've been floating above listening to all this, and I got to ask you, Max — was it worth it? Did you learn anything?"

"Well, there's definitely a ghost in that house, and I'm guessing it's Cal Baxter." With a deep breath, Max unloaded the whole story. He told of looking up the spell on the Internet, the weird voices he heard in his head, the images he saw, and the way it took him over, luring him into the circle. When he finished, he looked to Sandra and said, "I'm sorry. I shouldn't have done it."

Sandra held his hand against her chest, her eyes watering. "You are more important to me than anything. Don't do this again. I can't have you leaving me."

Max leaned over and kissed her. "I promise." He knew things were far from perfect between them, but this simple exchange eased their tensions for the moment. Most married couples he had known had something similar — a gesture, a phrase, something that said *We still love each other and we'll be genuinely nice right now, but later, this argument will have to be finished.* Often, when they found the time to finish the fight, one or both of them had figured out a simple, calm solution, and they never had to argue further. Max's kiss and promise gave them both enough room to turn their attention back on the things threatening them — Hull, Rolson, magic, witches, murder. The usual.

"Okay, okay," Drummond said. "The important thing here is that Cal Baxter is in that house, and it sounds like he's been bound."

Sandra let go of Max's hand and straightened her posture — all business. "I don't think so."

"You don't think it's Cal Baxter, or you don't think he's bound?"

"Both. First off, we were all in that room, we all saw that circle. That thing did not look like any binding curse I've ever seen."

"No offense, Doll, but there's more binding curses than probably anybody's seen."

"True, but this didn't share anything with being a binding curse — other than a circle."

Max said, "Okay. I'll buy it. But why don't you think it's Cal Baxter?"

"Because of the images you saw. If this had been Cal Baxter, why didn't you see anything that looked like Cal Baxter?"

"I don't really know what he looks like."

"I'm pretty sure he doesn't look like some horned-creature. And if it was Cal Baxter, why wouldn't he communicate easier with you? We had no problem with Drummond when he was bound, or any other ghosts we've seen."

"So what are you saying?"

Sandra paused, letting the weight of her coming words to press fully on Max and Drummond. "I think it's a summoned spirit. I think it is a creature that has been pulled into our world unwillingly and is stuck in that circle. When you touched the circle, you connected to it, and it's been trying to strengthen that connection ever since. I think it was trying, perhaps, to possess you, to take over your body, to somehow get out of the trap it's in."

Drummond pursed his lips in thought. "You're saying this is some kind of summoned spirit, trapped in the Baxter House, and you're getting all this because Max saw an image of a horned-beast?"

"Admittedly, it's a lot of speculation, but whatever is in that house, I'm sure it is not the bound ghost of Cal Baxter."

Max's face paled. "Is it a demon?"

Sandra shrugged. "I don't know if there's a Heaven or Hell, Angels or Demons, or any of that. I only know that these images are from something that doesn't want to be where it is, and it's trying desperately to communicate. Perhaps with good intentions, perhaps not."

"What do we do about it then?"

Drummond's face brightened as he clapped his hands, but Sandra spoke first. "I'm not sure. I think we should be cautious about going back to Baxter House until we know how that connects with everything else. Now, I looked into this NGFS — turns out it's a school called New Garden Friends School. A 'Friends' school, or 'Friends'-anything for that matter, belongs to the Quakers. They're the ones who founded Greensboro."

Max winked. "You're starting to sound like me."

"Just because I'm not yelling at you doesn't mean I'm not

still ticked off. Save the cutesy stuff for another time."

Crossing his hands in front of his chest as if to deflect an attack, Max tried to charm Sandra with his smile. When she merely stared at him with one eyebrow raised, he nodded his defeat and gestured for her to continue.

She held her look for a bit longer. "NGFS Upper is a private high school and a middle school. The Lower school — K thru sixth — is near Guilford College, but the Upper school is in that field. They built a gymnasium a few years back. Before that, it was a different private school — might have been a special needs school, that wasn't exactly clear, and I couldn't get much more information — and before all that, it was a field."

"The photographs are of a field. Maybe it was an old farm at some point."

"Probably. Regardless, it doesn't seem to connect much to anything."

Drummond clapped his hands louder this time. "If you let me talk, I might have something to share. You know, something important."

Max said, "Hold on. Sandra, did you finish?"

She feigned a hurt look at Drummond. "I suppose so."

Max spread his hands in an expansive movement. "The floor is yours, sir."

Drummond rolled his eyes. "Well, while you were nearly getting yourself killed and the missus was finding empty fields with schools on them, I went ahead and found the witch. You're not going to believe this one — she's on our side."

"You're right, I don't believe it."

"No, really. She's a captive. Hull has her trapped there. She's a prisoner. When you saw her at the fights and she reached out for you, she wasn't giving you up. She was crying out for help. That symbol on her hand — she belongs to a group called the Magi group. They're an old organization, secret kind of thing, and get this — they are fighting the Hulls."

Sandra stood. "Are you serious?"

"Sweets, I would never joke about something like this. I'm

telling you, this Magi group has been around for over a hundred years. According to the witch, back in the early days of North Carolina, back when Tucker Hull broke away from the Moravians and started delving into magic, a group of people formed to fight back. Over the centuries they ended up with many allies. She claims one of them was O. Henry. I don't know if I believe that part, but they certainly named themselves after his story."

Sandra's face tightened again. "Where the hell have they been the last few years? We could've used some help. Now, they want to show up and screw with our lives like everybody else."

Wagging his finger, Drummond said, "I knew you'd feel that way, so I made sure to ask her. She told me that shortly before you two moved down here, William Hull had struck them a serious blow. It's taken them this long to recover. The way she looked when she spoke, I got the sense that this blow was more than financial — they lost the lives of people important to them. Anyway, the point in all this is that we've now got the best lead we have to anything. We got magic, we got Hull, and we got Rolson all wrapped up with this witch."

"Rolson?" Max said. "Is he still with the witch?"

"He's her guard and he's moved her to the O. Henry Hotel in Greensboro."

Max looked to Sandra. They both looked to Drummond. Max shook his head. "That can't be good."

Chapter 20

SANDRA WEAVED THROUGH the highway traffic as she soared down Route 40 heading towards Greensboro. The old car shimmied as she pushed seventy-five miles-per-hour. Max reclined in the passenger seat, his head still swirling from his recent experience with the spirit world. Thankfully, Sandra had the sense to send Drummond ahead to watch the witch and perform a little recon. For Max, it meant less talking, less wisecracks. From the glove compartment, Max pulled out a bottle of acetaminophen and took two of the white pills.

Sandra looked over. "You still feeling really bad?"

"I ain't feeling good, but I'll survive."

The way she set her jaw as she continued to drive around traffic told Max everything — he had not only been wrong; he had hurt her. It bothered him that he kept hurting her in his efforts to treat her well or to protect her. Perhaps she was right. Perhaps unilaterally trying to protect people only leads to their pain.

Max raised his seat and placed his hand on the back of Sandra's neck, stroking her hair and skin at the same time. "I am so sorry. I never meant to harm you."

"I know you were trying to solve the case in a way you thought was right, but that doesn't make it so. You have to realize there are more important things than solving a case or fighting the Hulls or any of this stuff. There's you and me."

"I do understand that."

"Really? Because your behavior often makes me think otherwise."

"Do you remember our third date?"

Sandra's face relaxed. "Of course I remember our third date.

It was the first time we ever had sex."

"Yes, but do you remember the date itself? I had planned out what I hoped would be a great evening for us, and though it did turn out to be a great evening, the plan never was. I expected to pick you up at six o'clock and take you to that awesome dive in Lansing — Carl's Corner. We would sit down and eat until the live band started up. Then I'd take you dancing. Afterwards, I figured we would drive around for a little until I got up the courage to invite you back to my place. Not a complicated date, but one that required a little bit of planning."

Sandra warmed at the memory. "I can hear you calling me on the phone, telling me that you were going to take me out to dinner and dancing. I was really excited."

"Well, it didn't quite turn out that way, did it? I picked you up at seven because I had a flat on the way to your house, then got stuck in a traffic jam. When we got to Carl's Corner, they were locked up and closed — health inspectors had shut the place down."

"You looked so ridiculous and cute standing by the door, reading the health notice and shaking your head. I think you figured the whole evening had been screwed over."

"You remember what happened next?"

"Of course. We went to Wendy's."

"We sat there for hours chatting away. No dancing. No music except for whatever crap they pumped through their speakers. Sharing fries, sipping pop, and happy as can be. One of the best dates in my entire life. It was that date that I really fell for you. Not to mention, that all happened before you suggested we go back to my place. And that date was the first time that I learned something which has happened over and over again in our lives together — that together we can take a bad situation and make it work; together we make wonders out of tough times.

"I mean, look at us now. We're living in a trailer, practically broke. But as tough as it is, as worried as I am, ultimately, as long as we're together, I know we'll survive. We'll be fine. So don't ever think I'm going to jeopardize that. The risks that I took — I didn't think they were going to be as serious as they turned out. I would never have done it if I had known what I was stepping into."

Sandra reached over and patted his knee. "You are so silly."

"I know. But I'm learning."

"Well, you better learn this one for good because I'm tired of having to prove it to you. Besides, our life is too dangerous for you not to figure this out. Now lay back, shut up, and get some rest. Things are going to get tough soon."

Max reclined and closed his eyes. The relaxed sensation washing over his weary muscles told him that he and Sandra had truly made up.

Twenty minutes later, he woke to find them zipping down Bryan Boulevard. Sandra nodded ahead. "We're almost there. What's the plan?"

Max stretched his body, feeling far better than he had in the last few days. "You and I are going to cause a big scene. That's the plan."

Chapter 21

FROM THE OUTSIDE, the O. Henry hotel stood like a giant box of brick and granite. Though less than ten stories tall, it looked as if someone had taken a New York City hotel, yanked it from the ground, and plunked it down in the middle of a Greensboro parking lot across from the Friendly Shopping Center (*Only a short distance from where Sebastian Freeman bought a house,* Max noted). The inside, however, proved to be an entirely different experience.

As they entered, Max immediately fell in love with the place. Dark wood walls, high ceilings, the earthy smell of a fireplace — like an old, dignified library with the atmosphere and aroma of a hunting lodge. To their left, they saw the reception counter. To the right, two brass elevator doors.

Walking ahead, the space opened into a large lobby. Thick, heavy furniture filled the area as classical music flowed around them. The ceiling rose even higher — a full three stories up.

Max and Sandra sat on one of the overstuffed couches and waited. Large windows formed the back wall looking onto open gardens with walking paths weaving through the foliage. The setting sun cast a golden hue across it all like a stylized painting. Max could hear the busy conversation of workers in the restaurant off to the right prepping for dinner.

With a sigh, Max leaned back, his eyes drifting up toward the ceiling. His breath stuck in chest. He couldn't believe what he saw.

Near the ceiling of the lobby, a huge green banner had been painted across all four walls. Written in golds and browns, Max saw the entire story "The Gift of the Magi" by O. Henry — his most famous work, and the one the witch's organization had been named after.

Only a few people stood around the lobby — a receptionist and a bellhop. Not a good crowd for causing a scene, but when the time came, Max figured he would do the best he could.

A half hour went by without any sign of the witch. Max shifted on the couch and Sandra patted his leg. He wanted to hurry the whole thing up, yet for the moment, he had no control over the situation. If only he knew what room they had locked her in, but he couldn't see going up the receptionist and asking for the room with a witch.

At length, Drummond appeared. "Good, you're here. She's coming down the elevators now. Rolson's with her and two ugly-looking thugs."

Max straightened but not out of anticipation. Rather, his brain asked him a question that shocked him — *Why here?*

As the elevator neared, Max's thoughts kicked into high gear. O. Henry had used a complex secret code for Cal Baxter. Without practice, nobody could create a secret code so complicated that it took three years to solve. Perhaps his other stories, perhaps other experiences — somehow O. Henry had learned this skill.

But then why use a secret code at all? Why not simply tell Cal Baxter directly? True, O. Henry was on the run from embezzlement charges, but surely he could have found some way to communicate with Cal Baxter.

Unless, both O. Henry and Cal Baxter were part of this Magi group fighting the Hulls. The witch had told Drummond that they knew O. Henry. Perhaps Cal Baxter was part of that group, too. Perhaps that's how they knew each other, and keeping their relationship secret might have been important enough to employ a coded message. If that were true, if O. Henry was involved directly with the Magi group, then this hotel might be something more than a place to spend the night.

Max looked up sharply at the Magi story. Could this possibly mean something more?

The elevator dinged its arrival, and Rolson stepped off with the witch in tow. On either side of her stood a burly man, all muscle and mean. Rolson wore a trench coat and fedora unknowingly mimicking Drummond. But whereas Drummond's outfit suited the man, Rolson's looked forced like a Halloween costume that didn't quite come together — particularly with his green sweater underneath. It would have been comical if not for the man's ruthless eyes.

Max's nerves awoke. He knew they needed to get the witch, but defying a man with a police force at his disposal did not sit easy. Then again, Max had defied the Hulls on several occasions, and that family had far more power than Rolson.

But I had something over the Hulls. That was a hard truth. He had no problem going up against the powerful when he had leverage. Against the Hulls, he had their journal that detailed many of their unsavory crimes and dalliances with magic. But against Rolson and the police, Max had nothing. In fact, in the seconds that Rolson stepped from the elevator, Max finally saw how the police thought of him — a suspect in a murder investigation, an overnight jailing for disorderly conduct, possible connections to an illegal fighting operation, and if made known, trespassing on a crime scene.

Max might have stood frozen in that lobby and missed his opportunity. Sandra saved him. She walked straight towards the witch with a loud, cheery voice and her arms open wide. "Momma! I'm so excited to see you!"

The employees at the reception desk glanced up at the sudden noise. Max hurried to Sandra's side. "We've been looking so forward to your visit. How was your trip?"

Ignoring Rolson's scowl, Sandra took the witch's arm. But one of Rolson's thugs pushed her back. Rolson thrust his hands in his coat pockets, and with smarmy condescension, he said, "I'll give a little credit for finding us, but you won't be taking her away. Look around you. Make all the noise you want. Nobody cares. You know why? Because I'm in control here."

Max glanced at the reception desk. The two employees had disappeared. No bellhops either. Apparently, everyone had discovered something important to do elsewhere.

"Get it now?" Rolson went on. "These people won't

sacrifice their jobs or this business to help you. They know who I am. They know the family I represent. They understand who's in charge."

Instead of swooping in or flying around the scene, Drummond stood by Max's side. His presence gave Max a bit of strength. "Don't listen to this bozo. If he really had that kind of power, he wouldn't have two hired goons with him. He'd have two police officers."

Though shaking inside, Max turned a firm glare upon Rolson. "I know the family far better than you do. And I know exactly what you are. So, I'll give you a choice. Hand over the witch and we go our separate ways in peace."

"That won't happen," Rolson said, his cold eyes dropping a few more degrees.

"Then I'll just have to take her."

"You'll be arrested."

Max peeked at Drummond. "I doubt that very much. Unless you want to explain in your report how you were connected to a woman practicing witchcraft for the benefit of illegal gambling."

This gave Rolson pause — and that pause gave Sandra a moment to act. She thrust forward, shoulder-checking the nearest thug in the gut. Taken off guard, the big man stumbled back a step. Sandra grabbed the witch and bolted for the closing elevator doors.

In that instant, Max knew she would make it onto the elevator as long as he bought her a few extra seconds. So he punched Rolson in the jaw. As Rolson fell, Drummond flew straight through the remaining thug. The cold and pain of having a ghost pass through caused the thug to yelp in a decidedly unmanly fashion. All of this gave Sandra and the witch the time they needed to slip into safety. The witch looked relieved as the elevator doors closed.

No time to cheer, though. Rolson and his two thugs had gotten back on their feet. Max whirled about and dashed off deeper into the hotel.

He weaved around the lobby's couches and chairs until he

reached the back end of the room. A bright hallway led further down. One side had all glass panels looking out into the gardens. The other side, painted white, had been decorated with ivy and mirrors. After the heavy, dark woods of the lobby, the brightness caused Max to squint as he ran.

At the far end, he saw a glass-paned door. He shoved it open and burst into a private meeting. Men and women in business attire sat around a conference table covered with papers and laptops. They looked at him as if he had spit in their soup.

"Sorry," he said as he dashed by, looking for an exit. The only door he saw led into the garden. He heard Rolson and his men rushing through the glass hall.

Max darted into the garden, straight across, and threw open the door leading back into the lobby. From the corner of his eye, he saw Rolson stutter to a stop and turn back down the hall. Max couldn't tell if his little maneuver had helped or hurt him, but he figured as long as they hadn't caught him, he still had a chance to survive this.

Drummond's head cut up through the floor, keeping pace with Max's feet. "Sandra and the witch went downstairs. They're holing up in one of the meeting rooms."

Max managed a nod as he gasped for air and sprinted down a hallway to his right. Doors lined both sides. Up ahead a cleaning cart blocked the way. Max barreled onward, hardly slowing down to slink by the cart, and rushed toward the end of the hall.

"Down here," Rolson called out, his voice followed by the thumping steps of his thugs.

Max's eyes darted from one side of the hall to the other, checking every door he passed. They all had numbers. One had the word ICE. He kept searching for the one he needed, even as he heard Rolson gaining ground.

Finally, he saw it — STAIRS. Max smashed his shoulder into the door, slamming it open, and stumbled forward. If not for his one hand accidentally banging the metal railing, he would have taken a horrendous spill — one that might have ended his escape. But his hand did hit the railing, and he grabbed it in time to guide the rest of his body onto the staircase with sure footing. He raced downstairs.

"This way," Drummond said, shooting ahead of Max as he led them to a door. The name *Medieval Room* had been printed on a simple doorplate.

Max jumped into the room and slammed the door shut — breathing heavy and sweating hard. Sandra and the witch huddled at the end of a long conference table. Medieval decor covered the walls — crossed axes, thick metal banding, even a complete suit of armor standing in the corner.

"What the heck is this place?" Max said.

Drummond said, "You really want to talk decorating right now?"

"Both of you be quiet." Sandra held the witches hand and leaned close to hear.

Max wanted to know what they were talking about, but that would have to wait. Rolson couldn't be too far behind. Surveying the room Max noted only the single door. Maybe he should grab one of the axes.

Reading his thoughts, Sandra said, "They're fakes."

"Then we've got to get out of here."

The door opened and Rolson stepped in. He brought a phone to his mouth. "I've got them. Get an elevator ready. We're coming up."

Max fumed. He hated the way Rolson's voice sounded as if the entire escape had been thwarted by his own hand. He hated the satisfied look on Rolson's face. Or the way that Rolson rolled on his heels like an enthusiastic Santa Claus bell-ringer — jolly, red faced, and chubby.

Rolson chuckled, and Max pictured him saying *Ho Ho Ho.* "When they told me you were not to be underestimated, that you had some serious fight in you, they weren't kidding."

No need to ask who *they* were. Max wondered if he would ever be done with the Hulls.

"I have to admit," Rolson continued, "even with their warning, I didn't expect you to be so much trouble. But now it's over."

"The hell it is," Max said and leaped onto Rolson.

Both Drummond and Sandra called out, "Max!" Sandra sounded worried, but Drummond's voice flooded the room with vigor and excitement.

In the instant that Max jumped into action, he had the satisfaction of seeing Rolson's shock. He wished he could stop things at that moment like a still frame at the end of some movies. But nothing stopped. Max careened forward and knocked the man against the door.

He shoved back, trying to gain a second to reset, but Rolson had some training — he didn't wait. As Max stepped back, Rolson moved in with a gut punch followed by an uppercut. Little lights sparkled across Max's vision as he tumbled to the floor. His chin ached and his eyes required a few extra seconds to settle the images around him.

Seconds he didn't have.

Though Sandra tried to intervene, Rolson shoved her aside with ease before straddling Max and punching him in the face. Those hammy fists slammed into Max's cheeks twice. As Rolson pulled back for a final, devastating blow, his face took on a horrified, painful twist. Though Max couldn't see clearly, he knew the answer — Drummond.

Rolson fell to the side giving Max a chance to get back up. Drummond let go, rubbing his hand and wincing, while Max steadied himself. Without hesitation, Max kicked Rolson in the side. Then he kicked again. And again. He only stopped when the door opened and a middle-aged waiter entered the room.

All eyes turned on the waiter. The dignified man stared back with his salt-and-pepper hair lending a sense of propriety to an otherwise chaotic moment. He glanced down at Rolson, stepped close in, and punched hard enough to finish the work Max had started. Rolson was unconscious.

The waiter offered his hand. A small tattoo had been inked between his thumb and forefinger — a circle with a swirling yin-yang symbol. "My name is Samuel. Thank you for helping our Mother."

"Mother?" Max glanced over at the witch. "Who are you people? What is this all about?"

Samuel patted down Rolson, removed a handgun from the trench coat's pocket, and said, "In the future, you should know that as long as Mother Hope is here in the hotel, she can come to no harm. That's why we made sure she was here."

"Made sure?"

"Max — may I call you Max? — everybody talks to everybody. The moment we knew Rolson had taken Mother Hope, we understood that he did so without the authority of the police. Thus, he could not bring her to jail. He needed a place to house her. We alerted all our friends at every hotel in the area, assuring that none would give him a room. When he finally called the O. Henry Hotel, he happily found a room available — exactly where we wanted him. This hotel is our central hub of control — our headquarters, if you will."

Max looked to Sandra. "Do you understand any of this?"

"Some," she said. "I'll explain in the car. Right now, we've got to go."

"Hold on. Go where?"

"New Garden Friends School. While you distracted Rolson and had him running all over, I've been talking with Mother Hope. I know where we need to go, so let's go."

Rolson stirred and moaned.

The waiter said, "Please listen to your wife and go. I don't want him to wake with you or Mother Hope in this room. If that happens, I'll be forced to kill him, and I don't want that."

Drummond descended next to Max. "Come on, Max. These aren't people to mess with. They clearly know things we don't, and well, frankly, when you're given an easy out like this, you should take it — most of the time. Anyway, this is one of those times."

Max backed toward the door. "What about Mother Hope?"

The door opened and two maids entered the room. With swift, economical motions, they helped Mother Hope to her feet and escorted her out the door. Sandra followed behind until she reached Max. She looped her arm around his and patted his shoulder.

"Trust me," she said.

"I do."

"Then we need to hurry. Pretty soon, Rolson will be back on his feet and he's going to be angry."

Chapter 22

MAX HAD SEEN SANDRA DRIVE FAST BEFORE but never like this. Traffic on Bryan Boulevard was heavier than usual, but Sandra weaved in and out with expert skill like she had been born for Nascar. Max sat in the passenger seat feeling worse than he had on the previous drive. His bruised cheeks promised to swell up as his eye blackened.

"Slow down," Max said.

Sandra pressed harder on the gas. "Rolson's not out of this yet. He'll try to come for us, so we've got to get to that school first."

"She's right," Drummond said from the back seat. "I take it the witch told you where in this school we're supposed to be finding the gold."

"She told me a lot more than that." Sandra pointed to the folder of Sebastian Freeman's photographs sitting in the door pocket next to Max. "Look through those. We've got to find where on the school property this thing is buried."

"Wait, you said — so she didn't tell you where?"

"There was only so much time with Rolson chasing you and all that."

Max said, "What exactly did she tell you?"

"She told me this Magi group exists not to fight the Hulls specifically but to fight any who try to abuse magic. That they're a secret society who keep to the shadows, keep quiet — I get the sense they're more secretive than the Hulls."

Drummond ignored the photos. "We already know this stuff. I'm the one who found it out the first time."

"I'm telling you what she told me. I figured hearing her say some of it again was like the way the cops will ask the same questions over and over looking for a slip-up."

"That works when you've got hours to interrogate a person. We need answers fast."

Max opened the folder and brought some of the photos closer to his face. "Will the two of you stop it? We've got enough problems."

"She started it."

Together Max and Sandra said, "Shut up."

Drummond crossed his arms and looked out the window. In a lower tone, Sandra went on, "The witch told me that they've let us do a lot of the public work, but they've been watching us and they're happy to use us whenever it suits them."

Max shook his head. "Great. Another bunch of people willing to use us."

"This school isn't that far ahead. We're not going to have much time."

"To do what? You don't really think we're going to find that gold. It could be buried anywhere on that property."

Sandra swerved into the left lane and received an angry honk from a rusting pickup truck. "The witch said we could find it and I figured Sebastian knew something about it, too, because he took pictures of the place."

Max rifled through the remaining pictures until he found a handful marked *NGFS*. The photos depicted three single-floor brick school buildings. Two of the buildings were up front with a walkway separating them down the middle. In the back, a large building rose above. A small parking lot covered the front, and ball fields had been placed off to the left. A second photo showed empty, untamed grassland.

Drummond pointed to the empty photo. "It's got to be in there. Why else would Freeman have a picture of that field?"

"It's a pretty big field. We're going to be digging all night long."

As Sandra headed toward an exit marked PTI Airport and Old Oak Ridge Road, she said, "Sometimes, you boys can be so stupid. Pull up the school's website. Check out the field in there. There has to be a school map or something."

Max brought out his cell phone. He tapped in the website and started clicking around.

"Hey you mentioned this."

"What?" Sandra asked.

"Didn't you say they built a gymnasium a few years back?"

Drummond inched closer but his cold presence caused Max to involuntarily shiver. "You found something?"

Max lifted the photograph. "Where do you think they built it?"

Sandra turned onto Old Oak Ridge Road and drove by many homes and a supermarket. "The witch spoke in very broken phrases. I don't know if she was all there or not, but she said the words *Wood* and *Three* over and over again. Wood-Three. Wood-Three. Maybe that has something to do with this."

"Sheesh," Drummond said, thrusting back into his seat. "You think you could have mentioned that a little earlier?"

"Sorry. I'm not used to driving this fast and having to solve a mystery at the same time."

Max put his hand up between them. "Don't you two start. We know this thing is probably buried somewhere under that gym, and now we have this information about *Wood* and *Three.* It's a gym — there's a lot of wood on the floor. I'm guessing it's over there. We'll figure out the rest when we get to the school. How much longer until we get there?"

Sandra pointed to an electronic sign on the side of the road that read — WELCOME TO NEW GARDEN FRIENDS SCHOOL.

Max looked at the sign and said, "Oh."

Chapter 23

The New Garden Friends School had been built off of Pleasant Ridge Road. It was a small private school consisting of three buildings and an open layout like a mini-college where students walked between buildings to get to classes. The newly constructed area sat in the back. Evergreens lined both sides of the school like stolid sentries watching over while creating a protective wall of green.

Sandra parked near the entrance to the building on the right — a large black letter 'A' next to the door. The building on the left had the letter 'B'. She assumed the gymnasium in the back had a 'C' somewhere near its entrance.

Though the evening traffic had slimmed, cars passed down Pleasant Ridge Road every so often. Some turned into the housing development across the street, but none slowed down to look at the school. Max guessed that seeing a car parked at the school, even at night, did not arouse suspicions amongst the locals. They would think that a teacher or the principal had worked late, if they thought about it at all.

Max and Sandra started down the concrete path between the buildings and headed toward the gymnasium. The temperature had dropped, and Max felt the inside of his nose freezing up.

"I'll see if I can get the door open," Drummond said and flew ahead.

About halfway down the path, a brick overhang formed a square area near a side door into the 'B' building. Something large and dark sat in the shadows formed by the back corner of the overhang.

"What's that?" Max asked, putting his arm out in front of Sandra — a useless but protective gesture.

Sandra pulled out a small penlight and turned it on the shadowed area. Max jumped at the sight of a bear. Only when he heard Sandra's giggles did he realize that the ferocious animal had not moved nor made a sound. Sandra walked over and knocked on the wooden statue.

"Guess they're the New Garden Bears, huh? You're lucky they weren't the panthers — that would've terrified you."

"It's dark, and I've had a crappy day. Give me a break."

"Come on. Let's go to the gym ... scaredy-pants."

Max kept his retorts to himself as they crossed a small courtyard to the glass doors of the gymnasium. Drummond waited inside, hovering by the door.

"I can't unlock it," he said. "The door has bolts in the top and bottom and a key lock flush with the surface. It's not like a house where I can turn a knob or switch."

Max looked off to both sides. Another door was at the right end, but he figured they would find the same situation. "What if you freeze the lock?"

"And do what then?" Drummond asked a bit sharply. Max understood — because touching the corporeal world caused a ghost pain, Drummond didn't want to do so unless he had a good reason. If he could open a lock to help the team, he would do it without question. But in this case, they had no idea what would happen after freezing the lock, and Drummond had no desire to suffer for nothing.

"We could smash the glass," Sandra said.

Max put his face close to the door. "I can't tell if the doors are alarmed or not. At the least, they probably have a sound detector that would pick up shattering glass."

Drummond clapped his hands. "Then we make sure it doesn't shatter." He placed his hands on the lower pane. With a nod, he allowed his ghostly hands to become tangible. He kept them on the glass, wincing at the sharp pains, as he focused on the task.

The glass frosted over. The frost whitened and a crack appeared. Then another. The cracks grew, splintering off until they connected and formed a drunken spiderweb.

Drummond removed his hands, visibly relieved, and gestured toward the door pane. "Be my guest."

Max took the penlight from Sandra, and with the back of it, he poked gently at the cracked, frozen glass. Pieces fell apart like hard candy. The small chunks dropping to the floor made a soft tinkling sound — nothing loud enough to set off an alarm.

"Good job," Max said.

"I live to serve."

"You're dead."

"Then shut up and get in here. We've got some gold to find."

Crouching down, Max and Sandra stepped through the bottom part of the door. The bits of glass gave off the chill of a ghost cold enough to notice even in the cold, night air. They entered a small lobby, their footsteps echoing off the tile. As a teenager, Max had dreamed of breaking into his high school, but doing it for real lacked the thrill he had expected.

Probably has to do with the fact that my life is being threatened.

To his left — a glass-walled room filled with musical instruments. To his right — a small kitchen with a concession stand window for sporting events. Also on the right, he saw a long hall that led far into the back. Student-made sculptures and paintings lined the walls.

Peeking over Max's shoulder, Sandra said, "Looks like they use this for more than just sports. Art, music — I wonder what else is down there."

Drummond said, "Doesn't really matter what they use the building for. Can we focus on why we're actually here?"

Max looked ahead at a trophy case on the back wall. Basketball appeared to be one of their big sports. To the left of the trophy case, he saw double doors that led into the gymnasium.

As they entered, the heavy odor of wax assaulted his thawing nostrils. Max had not been in a gym since his high school days, and even the sound of his shoes on the floor rushed the memories back. He could almost hear the steady ringing of a rubber kickball bouncing on the floorboards.

"Let's spread out and look around."

By "spread out," Max meant for Drummond to go off in one direction while he and Sandra went another. They only had the penlight to guide their way, and without that light, they would be standing in total darkness. Drummond, as a ghost, had no need for light. He saw better than a cat.

Moving along the perimeter of the gym, Max whispered, "How are we ever going to find anything? We can barely see a few steps in front of us."

"We'll find it," Sandra said. "Remember the witch said *Wood* and *Three*. It's a good bet the wood has to do with gym — I imagine it's the only wood in this building. So let's look for things that come in sets of three."

"It won't be basketball hoops. There are six of those."

Sandra flashed her light up but the weak beam could not reach the nets. They walked by an entrance toward the locker rooms.

Max pointed in. "There're only two of them."

"Yes, but the number three is on lockers. Maybe it's there."

"I doubt there's been gold hidden for years in one of the lockers. If there was, then why would Sebastian take photographs of any empty field?"

"Maybe it's *under* a locker with the number three on it. You know, under the ground."

Max poked his head into the locker area. "Concrete floor, hon. Not wood."

Before Sandra could snap out a sarcastic rebuttal, Drummond's voice broke through the darkness. "I found it!"

Max and Sandra locked eyes like a sitcom married couple before dashing across the floor. Three quarters of the way, they found Drummond pointing to the floor. "It's the three-point line."

Tense from the run, Max said, "Are you kidding? It could be that, but there are plenty of things that have got the number three in it."

"I already checked underground. There's a box a few feet down. We've got to start digging."

"Oh," Max said with dumbfounded eloquence. "I guess I'll get some tools."

In a flurry, he rushed back to the car. His heart pounded at the thought that they might be on the verge of huge riches. He popped the trunk and pulled out flashlights, a pickaxe, and two shovels. It no longer bothered him that he carried these things in his car. Working so often with the dead made such tools mandatory. It bothered him now that it didn't bother him at all.

Careful not to drop anything, he hauled the cumbersome tools back to Sandra and Drummond. All the time, he promised himself that he would add a carrying bag to the equipment in his trunk. Just what he needed — more specialized stuff.

With a loud clatter he dropped the tools on the gymnasium floor. The sound echoed off the walls, and Max cringed. He did not bother looking at Drummond or Sandra — he knew the scowls he would see. Instead, he listened for an alarm to be triggered.

When nothing came, his shoulders lowered and he let out a sigh. "Sorry."

"It's okay," Drummond said. "We're going to have to make some noise to dig up this place anyway."

Sandra picked up the flashlights and illuminated the area that Drummond had indicated. Max lifted the pickaxe and wasted no time in breaking open the expensive waxed floor.

"How much gold do you think is there?" Max asked Drummond. "I mean how many chests?"

"I only saw one, and it didn't look too big. But, hey, one gold bar for free is better than none."

Max slammed the pickaxe into the floor again, wood splintering up and out. Sandra took a shovel and pried open a larger area.

"One box? Are you sure?"

"I'm sure. Don't worry, kiddo, whatever's in there, it's what we came for."

As Max continued to dig, his mind weighed out Drummond's words. With enough money, the problems with the Hulls no longer existed. If the Hulls could buy protection, so could they. They didn't even need to be as wealthy as the Hulls — only enough to protect themselves. And even less than that would be fine.

Enough to get out of the trailer and into a house, enough to pocket away so that they could continue their work without fear of being unable to put food on the table or pay their bills, the ability to have a decently heated room — any of that would be nice. One gold bar wouldn't do it. One chestful — that might be enough. It depended on how much gold traded for, and Max had no clue.

Then again, Max reminded himself, whatever they uncovered was found money. Even only ten dollars meant ten more than he had in his bank account. Though his muscles already complained, he quickened his pace.

Max and Sandra had stripped past the wood and reached the concrete slab foundation. Max attacked the slab, lifting his pickaxe into the air and letting gravity slam it down. Within a few strikes, his body broke out into a sweat. A few strikes more and he had soaked through his clothes.

Wiping his brow and panting heavily, Max said, "I can't imagine having to do this all day."

He picked up one of the flashlights and shined it on his work — barely a dent. He didn't need to look at Sandra to know the disappointment she felt. He felt it, too.

Drummond glanced down the hole. "You got anything stronger in your car trunk?"

"No. Haven't had to dig through concrete before."

Sandra said, "This is going to take too long."

They stood around the hole, staring at it like cavemen unable to figure out why their fire went out. Max kept waiting for a solution to flash in his mind, but nothing came. This couldn't be it. He refused to accept the idea that they were standing atop riches he could not reach.

"Maybe I can do this," Drummond said, leaning closer to inspect the hole.

Max said, "How? You can freeze concrete?"

"Don't know until I try."

Drummond pulled his arms back, ready to thrust them into the concrete, when Max said, "Wait. Isn't this going to hurt you?"

With an incredulous tone, Drummond said, "Of course, it's going to hurt me."

"I mean more than usually. I mean permanently. If you were alive, I'd be worried that it'd kill you."

"I don't know what it's going to do to me. But we can't just stand around here staring at this thing."

Sandra took Max by the arm and pulled him all the way to the wall. Drummond remained by the hole, cast in the dim flashlights, looking like a weary cowboy staging a bizarre camp scene in the middle of a darkened forest.

"Wish me luck, Doll." Drummond's voice echoed toward them.

Sandra blew him a kiss. "Good luck."

Max wanted to stop Drummond but knew the ghost would not listen unless a good alternative could be presented. Max had nothing to offer. He watched as Drummond jerked his arms into the concrete and cringed at the sound of his friend screaming.

After a few seconds, the screaming intensified — loud yet trailing off quickly. Max's mind had a hard time reconciling the dampened sound occurring in a cavernous, echoing gymnasium. Drummond cried out again.

Max stepped forward, but Sandra pulled him back. She hugged him. Her arms were warm, and against her, Max could feel his own body tremble.

She kissed the side of his face, and in his ear, she whispered, "Even if you went over there, you couldn't do anything. You can't stop him. And if you touch him, you'll only make his pain worse."

Drummond's screams continued. Max wanted to clutch his ears, to drown out the sound, yet at the same time, he thought it was his duty to listen — to offer that little bit of support when he could do no more.

And then it ended.

Abrupt silence cut through. No tapering off of agonized cries. Just sudden quiet.

Max and Sandra rushed over. They found Drummond floating listlessly nearby. His body slumped over. His arms dangled in the unseen currents of air above.

Max had to drop to his knees in order to see Drummond's face. "You there? Are you going to be okay?"

Drummond groaned and in a weak voice said, "Never better."

Max heard harsh scrapping to his left. He looked over and found Sandra shoveling out chunks of iced-over concrete. Max sat back astonished.

"You really did it."

She scooped up another shovelful. "Yes, he really did. Now get up and help me."

Smiling, Max grabbed the pickaxe and broke apart the last of the concrete. Soon, they dug into dark soil. Within ten minutes, Sandra's shovel clanked against something metal.

The excitement of their goal being so near fueled their energy. Max and Sandra dug furiously until she was able to reach down and remove a small, rusting box.

Max knelt before the box while Sandra played her flashlight upon it. Even Drummond perked up at the sight of their success.

The box, no bigger than a fishing tackle box, had a small clasp on the front and no lock. Max flipped it open and pushed back the top. It gave way with a soft whine. They all leaned over to peer in.

No gold.

Max reached in and pulled out a piece of paper folded over several times. Unfolding the paper, it opened into a large blueprint.

Sandra pointed to the paper. "Is that this school?"

"No," Max said. "This is Baxter House."

Though weak, Drummond managed to point to the bottom corner. "Might be the original. Look here."

Checking out where Drummond had indicated, Max saw in the information box that this architect's blueprints were based upon *the specific instructions of Mr. Cal Baxter.*

"This is it. The real thing. And look here. That's the secret room attached to the study."

"That's a lot of floors underneath it."

"Looks like the secret room had more secrets to give. Want to bet that somewhere down there is the gold? Or at least instructions on where to go to get the gold?"

A familiar voice spoke out of the darkness. "That'd be a good bet."

Max recognized Rolson's ugly tone right away. He turned his flashlight onto the man. Rolson stood with his feet wide apart. In one hand, he held a gun with a bright light mounted on top; the other hand, he held out, palm up.

With his light blinding Max, Rolson said, "Take your flashlights off me."

Max and Sandra complied. It was difficult to argue with a gun.

"Now, fold that blueprint back up and hand it over."

Max took his time folding the paper, trying hard to memorize what little details he could.

Sandra said, "You know you're nothing but a pawn to them, right? The Hulls. You get them this gold and they'll dispose of you. If you're lucky, they'll kill you. If you're unlucky, you'll end up being a magic experiment for them."

"We're all pawns, honey. The Hulls, the Magi, witches, covens — you been here long enough to know that much already."

"You're only a pawn if you let them use you like one."

"Give me the blueprints or I'll show you what this pawn can do with a bullet."

Max jumped to his feet. "Everybody calm down. Here's the map. Go in peace."

"Peace? You hurt me. Where was the peace in that?" Rolson snatched the paper from Max's hand and stuffed it in his trench coat pocket. But he didn't leave. Instead, he paced a wide circle around them, always keeping his gun fixed on them, growing angrier with every word.

"You've got the blueprints, now. We're beaten and tired. We can't do anything more. So, you win. Go. Get your gold."

Rolson sneered. "We had peace until you came along. The Hulls, the Magi — sure they're warring with each other, but it's a quiet, secret kind of war, it doesn't flow over into the daily lives of the people of Winston-Salem and Greensboro and the whole Triad. But you come along, and Sebastian Freeman, with your questions and your arrogance, and you disrupt everything. All these years, all I ever had to do for the Hulls was to occasionally bury an arrest or misplace a bit of evidence. Nothing so terrible that I couldn't sleep at night. Ever since you showed up in Winston-Salem, I've had to be on the move. I've had to deal directly with witches, falsify reports, and hurt people. I've managed to stay in the shadows, keep eyes off of me, but I was there, and now with Freeman and Baxter House and you, this pawn became a much more important piece on the board. So, thank you, you bastard. Thanks for screwing up my life."

Max squinted at the blinding light in his eyes. "We didn't come down here to screw anything up. The Hulls brought us here. They screwed things up for you."

"Shut up. I don't care who brought you here or why you came. All I know is that the two of you have caused me more headaches than an entire lifetime living here. And now let me tell you something — I want out."

Max's head perked up. "The gold — you want it for yourself."

"That's right."

Though speaking with a lethargic drawl, Drummond managed to say, "Careful, Max. I've heard men talk like this before. He isn't stalling for time and this isn't part of his mission. Speeches like this, this guy, he's building up the courage to shoot you two."

Max agreed. The way Sandra clasped his hand tight suggested she had come to the same conclusion.

Rolson whipped his head around in spurts as he spoke, disheveling his hair, while all the time maintaining his circular path. "Why shouldn't I take this gold? They don't need it. Heck, they don't even want it. They only care about the stupid chest it came in."

"But they're not going to let you take that gold, and you know it. They'll hunt you. For the rest of your life, if they have to."

Rolson stopped, and the corner of his mouth rose slightly. "Oh, I got that all figured out." He raised his gun. "And it all starts with you two. Right here."

"Listen. We can work a deal. There's no need for this."

Rolson's face deformed as he tightened all of his muscles. In a low, calm voice, he said, "Burn in Hell." Then he fired the gun.

Max saw the flash of the muzzle and thought how bright it appeared in the dark gym. Like a camera flash or a bolt of lightning, it lit up the entire cavernous gym for less than a second. By the time the sound of the gunshot reached Max's ears, he should have been dead. He even had time to notice that he had not died.

And in that rapidly passing second, his brain took note that despite all Drummond had been through, he had thrust his ghostly body in the path of the bullet, that doing so would slow down the bullet but not stop it entirely, and that Max should duck. Max did more — he dropped flat, pressing his face against the cold wood floor. Sandra lay next to him, offering him a smile that said simply — *I'm not shot.*

Drummond cried out. Not a painful cry but rather a war cry — he attacked Rolson. He tried to, at least. He flew in fast but slammed into an unseen wall.

Rolson stumbled back from the hit. Licking his lips, he pulled out a necklace with a small bag tied to it. "You think I don't learn my lessons? I may not be able to see you, ghost, but I know you're there. This here is a ward against you. You won't be hurting me ever again. You hear me?"

Rubbing his head, Drummond said, "Tell this moron I hear

him. Tell him anything, so long as he shuts up."

But Max had a different move in mind. While Rolson yelled at a ghost he couldn't see, Max and Sandra scuttled off into the darkness. Holding her hand tight with one hand, he kept the other in front, waving it around in the total darkness.

They moved slowly. Max could hear Rolson cursing Drummond and laughing at the same time. He had never seen a man go insane before, and he hoped never to see it again — at least, not when the man holds a gun. Max's hand bumped into something solid and wide. A stage. Like many schools, this one had built a stage at one end of the gym.

Speaking soft right into Sandra's ear, Max said, "Climb up."

Max crawled up onto the stage and felt Sandra behind. He slid forward until his head bumped a curtain. Finally, something had gone his way. Holding the bottom of the curtain up, he let Sandra crawl under and quickly followed.

The whole thing had lasted only seconds but to Max, it had felt like minutes. He couldn't understand why Rolson hadn't searched for them. As he let the curtain down, however, it became clear — despite the pain involved, Drummond had continued to attack Rolson's ward. He distracted Rolson, playing on the man's disjointed mind, and thus, giving Max and Sandra plenty of time to escape.

If you could drink, I'd buy you a lot of whiskey, my friend.

Sandra latched on to Max's hand again, and this time, she led the way off the stage. They bumped into a few chairs, but she found a set of stairs that led them into the far end of the hallway. Straight ahead, they found a door leading outside.

"Where the hell are you?" Rolson bellowed.

"Go," Max said.

They bolted to the door, slammed it open, and didn't stop. Max pointed toward the line of evergreens up a short hill. Sandra nodded even as she sprinted ahead. When they reached the trees, they ducked beneath the thick branches and scurried close to the trunk of the nearest one.

Rolson stumbled through the door, his gun lolling to the side. His breath puffed out in the cold air. He looked drunk and confused as he twirled around, searching aimlessly for them. But Max didn't think the man to be as lost as he appeared. He may have fallen into a bit of insanity, but that only made him unpredictable, not unable to function.

With a sudden shift, Rolson stood firm and stared straight into the trees. Max stared back, refusing to move a muscle, promising himself that the man could not possibly see them. Sandra watched, too, also holding still. Neither of them dared to even breathe.

Throwing his arms out in disgust, Rolson grunted and stormed off to the parking lot. Max heard Sandra exhale and followed suit. They held still until they saw the lights from his car turn onto the main road and disappear.

As they emerged from the trees, Drummond flew out from the gymnasium. Though dead, he looked queasy.

"Stop hurting yourself for us," Sandra said, shivering in the cold.

Drummond forced a wink. "Who else am I going to hurt myself for?"

"I mean it. I'm going to feel guilty for long enough as it is."

"Sweet of you to say, but you got nothing to feel guilty about. You're my friends. Besides, it hurts but at least I get to take a jab at the Hulls — well, one of their little minions, anyway."

Sandra glanced off into the dark. "That minion is on his way to Baxter House to steal the gold. We've got to get going."

"Hold on," Max said. "We're not going to rush into this blind. We've done that enough for one day. It's going to take us forty minutes or so to get to the house, which means it'll take Rolson that long as well. That gives us some time to come up with a plan. Good thing with that is — I think I have one."

Sandra grabbed Max and planted a kiss firmly on his lips. "Let's hear it."

Chapter 24

SANDRA PULLED UP AGAINST THE CURB a few blocks away from Baxter House. With the details worked out, the last twenty minutes of the drive had been spent in silence. Only now, as they sat in the cold, Max saw that for Sandra the silence had been one of mounting tension. She gripped the wheel white-knuckle tight and her chin quivered as she stared ahead.

"I'll be fine," Max said. "This plan is a good one."

Sandra shifted her body in order to face Max head on. She reached over and took his hand. Her skin felt warm despite the freezing cold surrounding them. "Why are we doing this? Rolson has got to be there already. He probably has the gold. We've lost."

"Even if he has the gold, it doesn't matter. We have to go in there. We've got to stop him from getting away with it. And we've got to get that chest for Cecily Hull."

Sandra's thumb rubbed circles on the back of Max's hand. "This doesn't feel like other times. I'm worried."

"If we all do what we planned, I'll be fine. You'll be fine. It'll work. Besides, Drummond's already off doing his part. We can't leave him hanging alone."

Sandra looked down at their hands and said nothing. In the dark silence, Max felt her thumb moving over his skin. In response, his fingers danced along her hand. He could feel her fears and desperation all through that sliver of contact between them.

They had held hands many times in their life together, but this felt different. This tiny connection felt stronger than any other physical contact they had ever shared. It focused all they were about to face, all their thoughts and concerns, all their history and future — all of it wrapped up into one small touch. In the same way that a stubbed toe could be more painful than a broken bone, or that a brush of the lips could be more erotic than a deep kiss, Sandra and Max's clasped hands brought them closest to each other's heart.

Though her body had not moved, Max could tell that tears fell from her eyes. "What is it? What's wrong? Is it really this plan?"

"It's not the plan."

"Are you that scared of Rolson? We've dealt with tougher."

"I know. It's not that."

"Then what? Why are you so upset?"

With a sniffle, she said, "I want to tell you something that I've never shared before."

"Really? I thought you'd told me everything."

"Don't be like that now. I have an entire lifetime of things that I probably haven't told you. I'm sure you do, too." Sandra paused, her brow tight as she prepared herself. "This is about when we got engaged."

Sandra exhaled a slow breath. The longer it took for her to speak, the more questions Max's mind spun off. He couldn't help it — the thoughts simply popped in his head.

Had she cheated on him before they were married? Had she gotten pregnant and had an abortion without telling him? Was there some back room deal she made with the Hulls in an attempt to protect him? What could be so terrible, and what did it have to do with now? Was she clearing her conscience because she thought he might die this time?

Sandra brought her other hand over and held Max's between her own as if praying through his hand. "After our engagement, when I told my mother the good news, she begged me to break it off. She didn't like you. No, that's not true. She hated you. She said she didn't trust you and that you were no good for me and that you would only bring me pain. Of course, I told her what she could do with her opinions. But then, she said it was more than opinion."

"What are you trying to say?"

"That night my mother told me something I had never known about her. She confessed that like me, she had gifts. She was clairvoyant."

"Wait a minute. Are you serious? She can see into the future?"

"Something like that. She never would explain too clearly how it all worked. But she told me that she could see things for us and that what she saw was filled with struggle and sadness and pain."

"Well, we've certainly had our ups and downs. We've definitely had our share of those things. But I don't regret it. Do you? Is that what you're saying?"

Sandra's hands pressed tighter against his. "No. Never. I love you, and I don't ever want you to think that I would give up what we've had."

"Then why are you saying all this? What is this about?"

"When she told me all of this, there was a look in her eyes — a sadness unlike anything I had ever seen. I used to think she saw my death earlier than it should have been. But in the last minutes as we neared this house, it hit me strong — a feeling that matched how I felt when I saw her that night. I think her vision, her seeing into the future, I think she saw what we are about to do tonight. I think she knew the outcome would not be good. That's why I don't want you to go in there."

With his free hand, Max brushed away the tears from Sandra's cheek. "That was quite a story. Now let me share something with you about that same time. While your mother was talking with you, while she was planting these seeds of horror in you, your sweet father paid me a little visit."

"He did? Why didn't you ever tell me?"

"Because I didn't want to change the way you saw him, and because I didn't want to start off our marriage with what I'm going to say. See, he took me to a bar, sat me at the end of the counter, and got us beers. All very manly — just like your dad did everything. All designed to intimidate under the guise of camaraderie. I half-expected him to pull out a hunting rifle and set it between us. Anyway, he told me that he and your mother didn't want us getting married. He didn't like me, and he knew you could do better. So, he offered to pay me a lot of money to walk away."

"Are you kidding me?"

"You know I'm not. In fact, he said that if I wanted more, they'd even put a second mortgage on their house. Whatever it took to get me to walk away. Up until a minute ago, I had always believed that the offer had been made as a test. That he wanted to see how much I truly loved you or if I was really the kind of scumbag that would take such an offer. And now, I think he was serious. I think he would've paid me to leave. And I think your mother was every bit as desperate. They coordinated their efforts trying to get us to break up."

"You think she lied? That she wasn't clairvoyant?"

Max shrugged. "I'm saying that even if she was clairvoyant, she may have misrepresented the things she saw in our future." Max pulled Sandra's hands to his chest. "I hear you, honey. I understand your fears. I have them, too. But let me ask you this — what else can we do? Let's say I agree and we go home right now. Drummond will still be doing our plan. He'll be lucky if he's not caught by the Hulls and cursed again. And even if we somehow knew he would be okay, Rolson then gets the gold, gets the chest, and escapes. We still have to deal with the Hulls. I don't see any way for us to get out of this mess without me going down there and doing everything as we planned. If you have a better idea, please tell me, and we'll leave right now, we'll try to find a way to stop Drummond. But if not, then we need to set our fears aside."

"I know. I don't like being this way, but what my mother said way back then, it's just —"

"We don't know what it was. I do know that you're stronger than this. You've always been there for me, pushing me, telling me to be stronger for myself. Now, you need to listen to your own words. Take a breath. Shove these doubts aside. Be the woman I know you are."

Swallowing hard, Sandra nodded. "Don't worry. I know

what I have to do here. You can count on me. I'll get it done."

"I know."

Max lifted Sandra's hands to his mouth and brushed his lips across her skin. They looked into each other's eyes for a moment longer, and then he stepped out of the car. She drove away.

As Max walked toward the Baxter House, he tried to take his own advice. He worked to clear his thoughts and to focus on the task at hand. He had only seen a glimpse of those blueprints, but it had been enough to tell him that the rest of this night would not be a pleasant one.

Max clapped his hands once and rubbed them together. "Okay. Here I go."

Chapter 25

MAX HAD NO TROUBLE entering Baxter House — the front door stood wide open. Switching on the flashlight, he made his way toward the study in the back. Though he hadn't seen the House plans for long, he had seen enough. All those floors running straight below the secret room like a tower going in the wrong direction — Rolson had to be there.

The house seemed darker now, but that had to be a trick of lighting. Knowing this did little to ease Max's tension. He could feel walls of dark closing in around the flashlight's beam, crowding out any spill from the light, making sure Max could only see what lay in the beam's path and no more.

Walking deeper into the house, Max wondered if he should have brought a weapon. He knew Rolson would be armed, and there was that old saying about bringing a knife to a gunfight. What did it mean when he only had a flashlight?

Except that Max knew his level of skill with guns. He had meant to spend more time at the gun range, but practicing had never been his strong suit. Better that he didn't have a gun — he would probably end up shooting himself. Besides, Sebastian Freeman died in that study without a mark on his body, without any sign of cardiac arrest or illness or anything remotely connected to a normal, mundane way to die — evidence of magic. And with magic involved, guns rarely offered any help.

Max walked into the study to find the room illuminated by the black candle in the adjacent secret room. That lone candle provided enough light that he could turn off his flashlight, but Max kept it on anyway. He heard Sandra's warning echo in his head — better to be extra cautious, he decided. Besides, the last time he had been in this room, he knocked the candle over.

The candle gave off a musky aroma like a barn full of animals as its flame flickered off smoke. Rolson had been here. But even if the candle had not been reset and lit, Max would have known that Rolson had indeed come through because one of the seven painted doors had turned out to be real. Across from Max, a section of the stone wall stood ajar.

"Well," Max said, "at least you did the work for me."

He poked his flashlight into the dark recess of the open wall section. A narrow staircase spiraled downward like the stone stairs of a medieval castle leading to a dungeon. The walls looked cold and wet, and the dull odor of mold crept up from below.

Max looked back at the study. An odd sensation hit him as if he had been cast at sea and the study floated within reach — an island that guaranteed his safety. Or he could dive downward, cross his fingers, and hope that whatever lurked below would not kill him. All logic pointed to the safe island.

"But I'm dealing with magic, not logic," he said, allowing his voice to echo back into his ears.

He had to trust Drummond and Sandra. No matter what he found down there, he had to trust that they would do their part in time to keep him alive. He knew they would try, but that did not mean they would succeed.

Max swallowed hard and remembered the arguments he had given Sandra back in the car — he had to do this. If for no other reason, then to get them free of Cecily Hull. Crossing his fingers for real, he closed his eyes, and thought of Sandra. When he opened his eyes, he glared down the stairs with determination set in his heart.

And he climbed down.

With his flashlight held shaking in one hand, his other hand trailing the wall, he wished for a handrail and shoes with better treads. The entire way, which only comprised fifteen steps, felt like a treacherous journey along the side of a cliff. At the bottom, he entered a room shaped identical to the one above — including the circle painted on the floor. Unlike the other room, this one had no doors. He had no clue where Rolson had gone.

Max approached the circle, his heart hammering, his feet sluggish. He had no way of knowing if this circle held the same kind of power as the one above, but he also had no other ideas of how to move forth.

Three steps away from the circle, a gust of wind smacked him sideways. The air felt cold as if the gust came from aboveground, and as fast as it arrived, it disappeared. Max popped back to his feet only to get hit in the back with another huge blast of wind.

He spun around and headed back for the stairwell. The winds kept blowing from one direction, then another, with no perceivable pattern. They hit so hard, he could not make any forward progress.

The decision came fast — if he couldn't go forward fighting it, he'd have to go with the wind instead.

When the next gust came, this time from his left, he simply walked with it, letting it push against his back. It rushed on even heavier, lifting him up and hurling him against the far wall. There, he saw one source of the storm — vents had been built into the wall, flush with the surface, and painted to blend in.

Before the vent in front of him could shove him to the ground, Max grabbed a small lever at the side and pulled it down, shutting the vent closed. He saw the winds blow dirt by him this time, but none ushered out of the vent, none thrust him off his feet.

Staying close to the wall, Max walked around, shutting every vent one by one. When he finished closing the last vent, a door to another stairwell opened with a loud creak.

These stairs leading down to the next floor harbored all the cold, damp stone that the first set of stairs had, but these had a darker, more ominous aura about them. The walls seemed to suck in the light that Max shone down. And even noises sounded dampened and unwelcoming.

Halfway down the stairs, he heard the door above close and the winds started to blow again. A foul odor assaulted Max like a punch to the nose. Every step, the odor grew more pungent as if he closed in on a giant vat of excrement.

At the doorway, Max stopped. The room looked to be about twice as large as the ones above. An icy slush covered the floor — the source of the putrid stench. Another painted circle peaked out from beneath the odorous goo. Three wall sconces kept the room dimly lit. Running the perimeter of the room, Max noticed a narrow, stone rim that poked out. It led to a door on the opposite side. At one point, slush stained the rim in a splash pattern — it looked as if Rolson had slipped.

Max stepped out onto the ledge. He tried not to think of what horrible, disease-ridden foulness could create such a disgusting smell. With his back to the wall and his toes hanging beyond the edge of the rim, he inched his way along toward the door.

He took shallow breaths — only through his mouth. He kept his eyes focused on the door. As he stepped under one of the sconces, he heard the buzz of a fluorescent light. He stopped and peeked to his left — he had reached the spot where Rolson had fallen in.

He didn't want to chance stepping in the same place and meeting a similar outcome. No way would he be exposed to whatever concoction of ills formed that foul slush. Lifting his shaking foot, he stepped across and risked being unbalanced for a short time. Quickly he brought up his other foot and exhaled with relief as he slid along toward the door.

Standing in the doorway at the top of another spiraling staircase, Max paused to catch his breath. The smell kept him from taking too long, but his climb downward went slower this time. Despite the cold, sweat dripped off his chin.

At the bottom of the stairs, he found the entrance to the next floor blocked by a large rock. He turned his flashlight beam onto the rock's edges, tracing their path around the entrance. Near the top, Max noticed a chip in the stone. The closer he looked, the more he saw the white, chalkiness around the chip.

That's not solid stone.

Max set his feet in a wide stance, lowered his body, and shoved the large rock. It moved so fast, Max lost his balance and tumbled over. His shoulder banged into the wall, whirling him around and into the room. He tripped and tumbled face first into the stone floor.

Stars split across his vision. Blood dripped beneath his cheek, and his tongue could wiggle his left incisor back and forth. When his eyesight returned, he discovered that he had come to rest only two feet away from a corpse.

He rolled away from it, letting loose a girlish yelp, and did not stop until he reached the wall. Despite the aches in his face, he managed to sit up and glance back. The corpse had been there a long time — dust covered the clothing that covered the skeleton. Looking toward the doorway, Max saw what had tripped him up — the skeleton's foot. And around the ankle, he saw a gold cross. He glanced back at the arms — a Bible clutched tight against the ribs.

"Samantha Shoemaker," he whispered.

Back on his feet, Max inspected the room. Much like the previous rooms, this one had a magic circle painted on the floor. Large stones like the one he had moved dotted the edges. The only weird part — well, weirder than everything else he had experienced so far — shimmied under his feet. The floor.

It didn't want to stay in place as if the whole thing were floating atop a small sea. Based on what he had already seen, this didn't seem too far-fetched. He looked back at the open doorway, and an idea formed — one he thought quite bizarre.

He walked along the perimeter of the room, checking each stone for chips or cracks that resembled the one he had moved. None stood out, but he noticed that a thin crevice existed where the floor met the wall — or didn't meet. His idea solidified. He had to be right.

As he had done before, he set his feet firmly on the floor, put his hands on the wall, and pushed. The entire room moved like a giant merry-go-round. He held back pushing too hard, so the room moved slowly. He saw the doorway he had entered from disappear behind a wall of rock. Off to his right, another doorway revealed itself.

He shot out his hands and pushed in the direction opposite the room's movement. The stone wall concealed half of the doorway before Max's efforts stopped the room. He had enough space to slip through.

At the top of another set of stairs — Max shook his head and sat on the cold stone. He needed to rest. He needed to sleep for a week or two, but a few minutes would have to suffice.

Exhaustion made up part of it, but if he wanted to be honest, seeing that skeleton had spooked him. Not simply the unsettling sensation that often comes when confronted by such a thing, but it had reached deeper within, churning his guts with a primal force. He had felt that way as a child when he saw his first dead animal.

It was in the summer at a friend's birthday pool party. Robbie Horner — Max couldn't believe he remembered that name. At the party, Max and two other boys had been horsing around in the water when they finally heard the call for cake. Dripping wet with pruned fingers and shivering under their towels, the three of them headed around the house toward the front door to get inside. They could have easily gone through the back sliding door, but in their heads, this would be funny — and funny ruled over everything.

As they turned the corner, they found Mr. Horner standing next to a rose bush. Under the bush was a dead rabbit. Maggots squirmed all over its body — everywhere but its eyes. Those black beads stared out at nothing, had no life, but they bore into Max just the same. A breeze blew across and for the first time, Max smelled death. Before he knew it, he had run back around the house and puked in the pool.

Sitting at the top of a stairwell in the middle of a twisted mind's architectural nightmare, Max wanted to run off and find a pool to puke in again. What awaited him below now carried the weight of death in a way that had only seemed hypothetical before. Now, after seeing that skeleton, Max felt in his bones the reality of his situation.

He stood and shined his flashlight down. If Sandra and Drummond weren't busy with their part in all of this, Max might have turned around. But they were out there, and just as he counted on them, they expected him to do his best.

He opened his mouth, ready to yell down at Rolson in defiance, but he held back. This wasn't a movie or some stupid television show. Yelling out his position would only help Rolson prepare.

Instead, Max made a fist and knocked on the wall. It wasn't wood, but it was the best he had available for good luck. Then he moved on.

Two more skeletons littered the next floor. One stretched out across the painted circle. The remnants of a leather bomber jacket clung to the bones. The other draped over a series of holes dug into the stone — numerous necklaces fell beneath the rib cage. From these little bits that remained, Max felt sure he had stumbled upon Alex Crane and Ushiro Takashi.

Water spotted the stone, and near the doorway leading to the next level, Max saw puddles of blood with trails running off to a darker section of the room. Turning his flashlight into the shadows, he saw a third corpse — a large German Shepard.

Max tried to picture what kind of elaborate set-up Cal Baxter had envisioned for this floor, but all he could see was that Rolson faced off with a dog, won, and opened the next door — saving Max the struggle. Figuring the room might change and lock him in, Max rushed across the floor and onto the next set of stairs.

As he climbed down, he tried to recall how many floors there were. Cal had to have been insane to create this. Considering all the magic involved, every subsequent floor furthered Max's fears. If its purpose went beyond what he thought, then the true villainy below might kill him.

When he reached the next doorway, all doubt left him. Cal had been a bona-fide nutcase. The floor had been cut away, leaving behind a narrow, winding path across like a stone hedge maze in reverse. The gaps formed the magic circle, and Max thought if he fell down, he would find the bottom covered in painted symbols. But the truly insane part came a moment later. Flames shot up from below. They came in little bursts at seemingly random locations. Each time, the flames heated Max's skin no matter how far across the room.

If Cal really had been part of this Magi group, then they were probably crazy as well. He would have to be extra cautious dealing with them.

"You've got to survive this first." His voice bounced back at him, louder and more powerful — and he could hear his nerves.

Chapter 26

MAX STARTED ALONG THE PATHWAY AND fast found that it narrowed after only a few feet. With his arms spread out like a high-wire act, he tried to keep his eyes looking ahead. That was what people said to do — find a spot in the distance and use that to keep balanced. The biggest thing, the most important thing, he knew well — everyone knew it. *Don't look down.*

Little explosions of fire popped behind him and another off to the right. He kept his eyes on the doorway and thought of the next step, the next step. He pushed out all other thoughts — and there were many — so that only his balance, only his next step, mattered.

It worked. He had gone about halfway, and by focusing ahead, he had stayed upright. Even his nerves had lessened because he had kept his mind clear on the present task. He grinned.

And that tiny lapse in thought sent him reeling.

He flapped his arms, tilted to the left, shifted his body hard the right but overcompensated, and once he went over, he couldn't stop gravity. He looked in the direction of his fall. Two other narrow paths crossed like the parallel grating on an outdoor grill. Turning his body over, he thrust his arms and legs out forming a wide X in hopes of catching as much of the paths as possible.

When he hit the ground, his hand found one bit of stone to cling too — as did his foot and torso. A laugh erupted from his gut unbidden. He had survived. But as he pulled up onto the nearest pathway, a burst of flames rose beneath him.

For such a short duration, the ball of fire ate the air around him and forced his nervous sweat to evaporate. He stood and looked around. The heat continued to increase as did the strong smell of burning.

No pain. Just heat. *My jacket!*

Trying not to lose his balance again, he wriggled out of his burning jacket. A dark hole had formed on the back, its edges glowing as it smoldered a larger hole. Max tossed it aside.

"Damn you, Cal, I liked that jacket."

He remained on that path without moving for a full two minutes. Only when he felt calm enough to attempt the rest of the walk did he put out his arms, focus on the doorway, and begin again. When he reached the safety of yet another stairwell, Max leaned over and threw up.

At least going down the dark, stone stairways brought him one floor closer to being done. If not for that simple thought, his brain would have tried to talk him out of continuing. But surely he had gone more than halfway. To stop now meant returning — a longer trip than pushing onward. Besides, he and Sandra had made it through all their troubles by pushing onward.

When he entered the next floor, he questioned such an approach. Where the other floors had paint marking out the circle and symbols surrounding it, this floor had deep grooves. That would have been fine, but these grooves had been filled with a dark, crimson liquid. The smell of death hung in the air. Worse than a rotting rabbit at a birthday party, this death smelled stale, old, and full of pain.

Blood. The liquid had to be blood.

More disturbing — Max saw nothing else in the room but burning torches to light the way. No danger of any kind. And the doorway on the opposite side stood open and inviting.

Motionless, he observed the room. Nothing changed. He heard no threatening sounds, saw no threatening movement.

Cautiously, he put one foot into the room. Careful not to make any loud noises, he stepped ahead. Little by little he moved across the floor, avoiding the blood-filled grooves of the magic circle. When he reached the other side, he continued down the stairs at the same pace. Only when he could no longer see the light of the floor above did he resume a normal pace — and even then, he kept an ear open for any sudden change.

He should have kept an eye open. After having climbed down so many stairs, he took the rest of the stairwell for granted — but a sudden drop revealed three missing steps. Max tumbled downward, hit the next stair with his shoulder, flipped over, and rolled into the room.

He saw nothing. At first, he thought he had gotten turned around so hard that he couldn't focus but soon understood that the room lacked any light source. Reaching around for his flashlight, his fingers slipped into a slick wetness.

"Crap," he muttered.

Clenching his jaw, he tried to swallow back the urge to throw up again. He continued to feel around. There! His hand found a metal tube — the flashlight. Pulling it close like a parent protecting a baby, he whispered *Thank you* before flicking it on. Then he decided such thanks might have been premature. Sitting in the beam of light, he discovered the source of the slick wetness. His fingers had found a corpse wearing a torn hunter's cap — Alan Peck.

Whatever horror Cal Baxter had constructed for this room, Max decided not to find out. He shined his flashlight on the exit and discovered a clear path ahead. Crawling on the floor — partially due to the pain from his latest fall, partially to avoid any possible Cal-created surprises higher up — Max made his way across.

At the next set of stairs, he sighed relief. He knew right away this led to the final floor. Bright light cut through from below, and he heard Rolson grunting hard in time with rhythmic strikes of something heavy against the floor.

As he neared the bottom, the temperature dropped. An unnatural drop that Max had felt many times before — the presence of a ghost.

He entered to find a room identical to the one on the first floor — a simple, elegant room lined with doors and bearing a painted circle on the floor. A candlestick with a black candle stood in the center. The only differences — the floor had been made of wood and a thin layer of ice covered everything.

Rolson had taken a position putting the circle between them. He held a sledgehammer and sweat soaked his pasty brow. He winked at Max, raised the sledgehammer, and yelled as he slammed it down on the wood slats within the circle. The sledgehammer bounced but the wood remained intact.

Rolson laughed. "All we put each other through and this damn thing is sealed with magic. The ghost of Cal Baxter won't ever let go of his gold."

Max opened his mouth but did not speak. He couldn't. Behind Rolson, one of the doors had opened. A hard-looking man with close-cut hair, a pointed nose, and beady eyes entered. He wore a fine suit and appeared disgusted to stand in such a place. Max felt confident he knew the man, but all doubt went away when another man followed in close behind — Mr. Modesto.

"Mr. Porter. Detective Rolson. I believe you both know of Tucker Hull." Modesto gave a slight bow and gestured to his employer.

Chapter 27

ROLSON DROPPED TO THE FLOOR, prostrating like a zealot before his prophet. "Mr. Hull, I swear I'm trying with all the strength I have, but I can't break open the floor."

Modesto stood regal and snobby as usual. He stepped over Rolson as one might step over a rotting animal — careful and with disgust. Though his hair looked grayer than before and a few more lines marred his face, Modesto still carried the weight of his office in every over-pronounced syllable he spoke.

Max turned his attention to Tucker Hull. "Why the new body? Didn't like the one you stole when you destroyed my office?"

Modesto tilted his head back so he could look down upon Max. "Of all people, Mr. Porter, I would have thought you would take the time to do a little research on Mr. Hull. Had you done so, you would not bother with such a foolish question."

"Well, you know me — always the fool."

"Indeed. The process of maintaining Mr. Hull in this world requires fresh bodies from time to time. Nothing the Hull family's sizable resources cannot accommodate."

"And by *process* you mean *spell.*"

"Of course."

"And by *sizable resources* you mean all this gold you plan to steal."

Tucker Hull's eyes narrowed so sharp that Max felt a stab of pain in his chest. Those eyes traveled up and down Max, appraising him like an art dealer. Then Tucker walked forward — slow and strong. His voice matched. "I cannot steal what has always been mine. You are the thief here. But as the Lord would have it, perhaps one of His grand jests, I happen to require your unique thieving skills. Open the floor. Now."

Max pointed at Rolson's sledgehammer. "How can I possibly open this floor up when your own man can't do it with that thing?"

"Give me another chance," Rolson said. "I'm sure I can do it."

With an impatient fluttering of his hands, Modesto said, "Mr. Hull demands this of you, Mr. Porter. Refuse and he will be forced to send people out to harm your wife."

"I'm not refusing. Okay? Everybody just calm down. All I'm saying is that I don't know what you expect me to do that Rolson hasn't done."

Tucker moved closer to Max, but he approached in a slight curving pattern. *Trying to avoid the circle,* Max thought. Tucker stared straight into Max — the power behind those beady eyes burning through in an instant.

All at once Max was a child gazing up at a disappointed father, a dog fearful of its master, a young girl afraid she had misunderstood the glance of a boy, and a woman afraid she had understood the glance of a man. His head spun. Every cell in his body wanted both to run in fear and stay within Tucker's stare as long as possible. Intimidation and seduction — hand in hand — Max had never before experienced a person holding such power.

When Tucker spoke, however, the mesmerizing spell of his eyes broke. "Stop stalling. I do not expect you to use such a crude method as a sledgehammer. You are one of the few in the world that have seen, accepted, and appreciate the greater planes of existence around us — the places of magic and the supernatural."

"Hard to deny when I'm staring at you."

Tucker grinned. Max thought the man's teeth had been sharpened into points but Tucker's lips closed too fast to be sure.

"Clearly this is a problem of magic," Tucker said, "I expect you to find a magic solution."

Max turned to the circle, trying to control his shaking limbs.

In all the possible outcomes they had planned for, he and Sandra and Drummond had always expected Rolson to have already dug up the gold by the time Max arrived. Looking at the flickering black candle, Max wondered if this miscalculation would cost his life. Or, if Modesto's threats were to be believed — Sandra's life.

Rubbing his hands, Max said, "Okay. Let me think this through."

The floor couldn't be forced open because of a magic seal of some type — or a magic something. Tucker expected Max to open it. *Why me, though?* Tucker had access to the best witches in all of North Carolina — probably in all of the country, if not the world. Why not bring one of them down to break the spell?

Only one reason made sense to Max — Tucker couldn't. Not that Tucker couldn't get hold of the best witches, but rather that he knew they couldn't break the spell. Something unique about Max gave him, and only him, the ability. Otherwise, the Hulls would have opened the floor and taken the gold long ago.

But that posed a different problem. The Hulls had owned Baxter House for over a century. Even if they had not found the secret rooms until recently, they had to have been looking. They had to have been aware of the magical possibilities to protect the gold. All of which pre-dated Max's birth by decades. So, whatever was unique about Max had to have been able to exist before him.

That meant that it had to be something Max had learned or acquired or — Max's skin prickled as it clicked in his head. The magic circle. He had become connected to it. He would have figured it out sooner but, between threats from Hull and having faced the dangerous floors of Baxter House, his brain had suffered a bit of fatigue.

Crouching by the circle, he hovered his fingers over the paint. He had no desire to see that horned-creature again. But what choice did he have? He could only stall so long, and even if the rest of the plan worked, they still needed the gold.

Modesto stepped up behind Max. "My employer does not

have a lot of patience this evening. I strongly advise you to open this floor at once."

Closing his eyes, Max touched the circle. And nothing happened. He pressed his palm on the paint. Still nothing.

Straightening, Max winced at the idea forming in his head. He put out a hand toward Rolson. "Give me the sledgehammer."

Rolson lifted his head. "If you think you're stronger than me, you're crazier than I ever thought."

"Do as he says," Tucker snapped and Rolson moved fast enough to create a breeze.

Holding the sledgehammer, Max entered the circle. Again, nothing happened. Max frowned. He had expected something big — flashes of magical energy or bolts of lightning or a loud, ghostly thumping. But he recalled the way Tucker had avoided the circle. Perhaps simply standing inside unharmed proved enough of the connection.

Then his entire body seized. His muscles constricted, spit flew from his mouth, and his limbs shook. Instead of crying out, he could only manage a weak gurgle.

His head arched back. Floating on the ceiling, he saw the horned-beast. It pushed off and soared toward him. Max wanted to duck, but he had no control over his shaking body.

Except the beast did not touch him. It circled around him. The connection between them returned. Max's thoughts flooded with images — some his own, some from elsewhere. He saw birthday parties and children running in a field. He saw Sandra's joy as she held an engagement ring. He saw an ugly face lurking from a bedroom door and children throwing rocks at windows. He saw a train car full of gold.

Each image hit like a fist to the head. Yet Max endured — he had to make use of this moment. He had to stay focused. There seemed to be a pause between images, and when he felt the next pause arrive, Max did his best to form his own image — a message for the beast.

When his mind cleared, Max's control over his own body returned. He couldn't be sure that the spirit understood what he intended to do, but he hoped it wouldn't be angry with him. Only one way to really prove anything, though. Max raised the sledgehammer and brought it down on the wood inside the circle. It smashed through with ease.

Rolson cheered while Modesto offered a slight lifting of the lips. Tucker watched without expression.

Twice more Max brought the sledgehammer down. Twice more the floor gave way, sending splinters of wood flying off. Max peered down, reached through the hole, and pulled out a gold bar.

Dropping the sledgehammer in order to use both hands, he carried the bar outside the circle and placed it on the floor with a heavy thud. Tucker moved in close to the gold. "Get the rest."

Over the next fifteen minutes, Max brought out bar after bar. Forty bars in all. When he reached down and found nothing, he said, "That's it."

"The chest," Tucker said. "Where's the chest?"

Max pressed his face to the floor and peered in. "Nothing else down here. Sorry."

"Damn!" Tucker stomped over to Rolson and kicked him in the side. To Modesto, he said, "Get moving."

Modesto pressed his palm against a stone in the wall and a door slid aside. He rolled out a flatbed dolly and loaded it with the gold. As Modesto worked, Tucker glared at Max. Once the last gold bar clinked onto the pile, Modesto exerted all his strength to push the dolly through the door. He did not return.

"Hold on here," Max said, staring at the door in disbelief. "We could've all come in through there?"

With a mocking sneer, Tucker said, "You don't think I'd be stupid enough to go through Baxter's sick little maze, do you? You don't think Baxter would go through it, for that matter? Didn't you look at the blueprints?"

"I didn't have much time." Max shot a nasty look at Rolson. "What's your excuse?"

Tucker clutched his hands behind his back. "Don't feel bad. It was really a small note added to indicate the existence of a safe passage — not something drawn in. Most of the construction crew probably had little knowledge of it." He walked in front of Rolson. "Now, you have one last task, and after that, you may go wherever you wish, do whatever you wish, continue working for us or not. You will be a free man."

Rolson popped to his feet. "Anything. What do you want?"

"Kill Mr. Porter, of course."

Rolson raised his weapon and pointed it at Max. "On your knees. Slowly, now. No sudden movements."

Max lowered to his knees. "Come on. Be smart about this."

"Shut up. You've been a pain in my ass since I met you. Turn around. This has to look like a professional hit."

Looking straight at Rolson, Max said, "Have you been listening to any of this? There's a door that bypassed all those damn floors. They knew about it all along. They knew how to get down here but didn't tell you. You could have died on your way down, but they didn't tell you. Doesn't that show what they think of you? How can you trust them to set you free? How do you know they won't simply kill you next?'

Rolson lowered the gun a little. Max could see the doubts entering the old detective's brain.

Tucker snickered. "Mr. Modesto warned me how you think. Always accusing my family of the worst intentions. You think we murder people with ease. We do not. The fact that you've lived this long is proof. Rolson and those loyal like him are rewarded for their help, not punished. You, however, have not been loyal. You've tried to hurt us many times. And while we do not murder with ease, that doesn't mean we won't when necessary. All I see with you is one mounting trouble after another. This way is much better. Kill him. Do it now and you will walk away here owing nothing to Hull family."

Rolson raised the gun again — firmer, more determined. Max tried to find something to say that would stall the moment. Anything that might create a little time. But his mind went blank. He could only think of the dark hole at the end of the handgun — that soon he would see a flash of fire, and long before he heard a sound, he would feel his head crack back, and he would be no more.

His heart raced, and he put his hand to his chest. *Chest?* "Don't shoot. I know where the chest is."

Tucker leaped forward and shoved Rolson's gun out of the way. A bullet shot off digging into the stone wall. Warning off Rolson with a look, Tucker pointed to Max. "If you are lying to stay alive, you'll wish I had let Rolson shoot you. I can make you suffer greatly — and for far longer than is possible in the natural world."

"I have no doubt about that." Max paled with honest fear. Especially because while not technically lying, he hadn't really told the truth, either. He had *an idea* of where the chest might be, but he didn't know for sure.

"Speak quickly or your pain will begin right here."

Tears welled in Max's eyes. He knew he shouldn't say anything. To give Tucker Hull access to powerful magic was unthinkable. No better than handing an automatic handgun to a sadistic ten-year-old. Worse than that — Tucker would feel no remorse afterwards. The Hulls were masters of self-justification — and they all had learned it from the ancient, screwed-up mind of Tucker.

But if he didn't offer up something, he would be tortured — and eventually, he would spill what he thought he knew. The tears dribbled down his cheeks. This wasn't how they had planned things. Where the hell was —

"Drummond!"

The head of his dead friend dropped through the ceiling. As he descended, Tucker looked over and scowled. "You must be the detective that my children have complained about."

"Kids love to complain," Drummond said.

Rolson spun around. "Who the hell are you talking to? What's going on?"

Tucker slapped Rolson hard. "Do what I told you."

"They're going to kill me," Max said.

Drummond took one look at Max and said, "No, sir." He zipped across the room and body-checked Rolson in the back. Drummond shouted at the pain while Rolson shouted in surprise. The gun skittered across the floor.

Before Tucker could reach the weapon, Drummond moved in on him. Tucker stepped away and backhanded Drummond in the face. Both Max and Drummond stared in shock.

"You can touch me?" Drummond's hand brushed his cheek.

"Oh, you sad little ghost. I'm a soul brought back from the dead. I exist in both the living and dead worlds. I can touch it all. And I can make you hurt."

Tucker charged Drummond. As they grappled, Drummond screamed at the pain he suffered from the contact. But that didn't stop him. He punched Tucker in the jaw, sending the Hull patriarch flailing backward.

As the fight continued, Max saw Rolson inching toward the gun. "Fuck that," Max said and jumped on him.

Rolson had far more experience fighting, but Max had far more to lose. Desperation fueled him as he punched wildly into Rolson's body. After landing several strong hits, Rolson gave up reaching for the gun and rolled Max off of him.

Brushing off his shoulders, Rolson got to his feet. Blood dripped from his nose. He put up his fists and circled Max like a trained boxer.

Drummond and Tucker continued to grapple. They shoved each other against the wall and wrestled to the floor. Max watched as Drummond continued to fight despite the agony he wore on his face.

Rolson took full advantage of Max's momentary distraction. He came in at an angle with a haymaker to the head. At the last second, Max brought up his arms — not enough to block the blow, but he deflected a full-on hit to the temple. His head still took a nasty strike, shaking his brain, and causing spots to pop before his eyes.

While dazed, Rolson came in again. This time he kicked Max. Max fell over and clutched his shins. He felt the cool stone of the wall and realized he had no escape. A second later, Tucker threw Drummond right next to him.

All four men panted heavily. Tucker crossed his arms and said, "I think I'll forgo the torture and kill you both right now."

"I'm already dead," Drummond said with a slight groan to his words.

"Oh, there are plenty of deaths a ghost can go through."

Drummond got to his feet and Max followed. He looked down at Max with a questioning raise of his eyebrow.

Max wanted to smack the ghost himself. "I don't know. I've been down here this whole time. You tell me. Was that enough?"

Snatching the gun from the floor, Rolson said, "I'm so sick of you. What the hell are you talking about now?"

Max held onto the wall in order to stay upright. "Neither of you seem to have put it together. And here I thought at least one of you might have some brains." He gestured toward Drummond. "Didn't you notice that he's here? This ghost."

Tucker gazed upward. "You got the old Magi witch to break the seal against ghosts. So what?"

"Oh, she's doing more than that. She's up there with my wife, and together they've been breaking the seal on the circle itself. From the confused look on your face, I'm guessing Rolson here didn't bother telling you how he killed Sebastian Freeman."

Tucker's eyes leveled on Rolson.

"You said you didn't want evidence." Rolson squirmed.

"What did you do?"

Max tried to straighten more but the pain in his side prevented it — another broken rib. "He thought he summoned the spirit of Cal Baxter. He thought he sealed the spirit in this crazy place. All those magic circles line up like a telescope, each one making the one above stronger. But it didn't work."

"It did, too," Rolson said. "Baxter came and killed Freeman. You saw the dead body."

"Except that wasn't Baxter. Cal Baxter moved on when he died. Drummond had looked for him but couldn't find him because he's gone. You can't get to him."

"But I saw him. I saw him kill Freeman."

Tucker slapped Rolson on the back of the head. "Idiot. Cal Baxter designed these circles to be a strong prison to protect the gold from my family."

"Starting to see it now?" Max said.

Rolson looked confused and frightened. "I swear I saw him. He looked like a demon."

"That you definitely saw — but that wasn't Cal Baxter. That was Charlie McShay — the thief who stole the gold in the first place. How else do you think Cal found the gold? It took him a long time to realize that the message sent to him was simply Charlie's name. Cal had to learn the ways of magic on his own. Took him about three years until he felt confident enough to summon Charlie and force the spirit to help him get the gold. Once he had his riches, Cal built this place and locked Charlie up. That old spirit's been here for a long time. And he's angry."

"He's lying," Rolson said.

Tucker did not appear to agree. "He's connected to the spirit. That's why he could rip open the floor. That's why he knows all of this."

Max added, "We also couldn't find the ghost of Sebastian Freeman. My best guess is that McShay has kept him locked in this house with him. By now my wife and the witch have broken the seal and both ghost and spirit are going to be mighty angry. I think you ought to run."

Rolson pointed his gun at Max's head. "Bullshit." He pulled the trigger.

Nothing happened.

At first, Max thought Drummond had intervened again, but seeing the horned-beast — Charlie McShay — rise behind Rolson explained things. With a roar, McShay thrust a clawed fist into Rolson and lifted the man off the ground.

Rolson dropped the gun and shrieked. It lasted only a few seconds. He died fast.

Ignoring the beast, Tucker stomped over to the circle and grabbed the black candle. He muttered words over its light and his left hand began to glow ghostly pale. "You want to hurt my family? Is that what motivates you?"

McShay spread his muscular arms and bellowed loud enough to frighten a grizzly. Tucker raised his glowing hand

and shouted back. The two locked eyes for an instant before charging each other like jousting knights.

When they smashed together, a blast of energy brightened the room. The air whooshed out through the door. Sebastian Freeman appeared on the ceiling and Drummond dissipated, thrown into the Other — or so Max hoped. It was Max's last thought before falling unconscious.

Chapter 28

MAX PARKED THE OLD, BEATEN CAR next to the old, beaten trailer. He sat still, going over in his head how he wanted to handle the upcoming meeting. He couldn't afford to mess it up. Everything depended on success — possibly even their lives.

No, not possibly. Certainly.

When he had woken at the bottom of Baxter House, he found no sign of Tucker Hull. On the wall, however, he saw what remained of McShay — a silhouette of the horned beast burned into the stone. No sign of Sebastian Freeman, though.

Max clambered up the exit path, a winding ramp that took several minutes to reach the top. The door at the end led to the living room off to the side of the foyer. Sandra waited for him, ready to take him home.

Dawn arrived as they reached the trailer. By the time they had prepared eggs, toast, and coffee, they found a way forward. And they needed a plan. Tucker Hull was out there, livid at Max, and clearly capable of destroying a summoned spirit.

"This'll work," he said to the empty car before getting out.

Inside, Sandra had begun packing their things into boxes. She looked at Max with urgency. "You got it?"

He nodded.

"Good," she said. "I don't want to be unpacking this stuff right back into this trailer."

"We'll be fine. You heard from Drummond yet?"

"No."

When they first came home, Drummond had appeared and explained that the force of Tucker and McShay fighting had shoved him into the Other. When he found his way back, the fight had ended and Max lay unconscious on the floor. He flew up to Sandra, told her to wait, and then went back to the Other to heal up after all of the abuse he had endured. He still needed a good week off, but he had enough rest in the few hours away that he could still help them out.

After he had left for the Other, Sandra helped Sebastian find his way to move on. It was simple — he merely had to go to the Other and call out for Lilla. Together, they drifted away.

A knock at the door.

Max frowned. "Drummond's supposed to be watching Cecily Hull to warn us when she arrived. Where the hell is he?"

"Maybe that's not Cecily Hull."

Dread gripped Max's chest as he approached the door. What if Tucker had decided to finish off all the loose ends? Max might open the door and be gunned down by a hired goon. Or perhaps Tucker would do the job himself — far slower and more painful.

The knock came again.

Max opened the door a crack and peeked out. Mother Hope looked back at him. Not good. Not with a Hull on the way.

"What do you want?" he asked.

An arm reached around Mother Hope, and as Max opened the door a bit wider, he saw Leon Moore. "Merely to talk. It's cold out here. Please let us in."

With a gasp, Max opened the door and stepped back. Leon assisted Mother Hope up into the trailer and they settled by small table.

"To begin with," Leon said, "we wanted to thank you for your help in stopping Tucker Hull from acquiring any pieces of the chest. Items imbued with magic are dangerous in any hands, but in a Hull's hands — especially Tucker Hull — the results are not to be desired."

"We didn't do it for you."

"Regardless, thank you."

"Is that all?"

Leon bristled. "I know you might feel a little upset at my part in all this, but I never lied to you. I love research, and I am a librarian. My help was genuine. Now, considering you would be dead if Mother Hope had not aided your wife in breaking those seals, you're being awfully rude."

"I do appreciate what you did, but I don't think for a second that you did it for me. The only reason we even know your group exists is because we stumbled upon this old lady. And for that matter, you should thank us for saving her."

"We had her quite safe. In fact, there is no safer place than the O. Henry Hotel."

"Maybe so, but I'm still calling it even between us. You people — you're no better than the Hulls. You play games with our lives, hiding from us, popping up to mess with us, and I'm sick of it."

Mother Hope lowered her head. Leon said, "We are sorry to hear you feel this way. We had come here to invite you to join us." He looked at Sandra. "You both have great talents that we could use well. But clearly, you are not interested."

Sandra crossed her arms. "Clearly."

"In that case, we only ask that you do not interfere with us. If you can agree to stay out of our way, I don't see why we can't be peaceful towards each other."

Max gripped the kitchen counter while forcing a smile. "We've never wanted to be in the middle of any of this anyway. We simply want to run our little business, and live a decent life. It's you and the Hulls that keep dragging us into your mess."

Leon stood and tugged his shirt down. "Well, then, it's all very simple. Don't deal with the Hulls and all will be fine with us. I might even be able to help you out a the library from time to time."

Drummond burst into the trailer. He saw the witch and his ghostly face paled. "What's she doing here?" He took in the whole scene. "Oh, they've come to make a deal."

Mother Hope pointed at the ghost and Leon frowned. "Do we have a visitor?"

"No," Max said. "We have a partner."

Drummond smiled. "Thanks, Max." Then he leaned close and whispered, "Cecily Hull is almost here. You got five minutes, maybe ten if you're lucky."

Max offered his hand. "Stay out of our business, and we'll stay out of yours. That's the deal, right? Shouldn't be a problem. We'll stick to the Winston-Salem area, and you stay in Greensboro."

Leon looked to Mother Hope before shaking Max's hand. "You'll find the cities are closer than you think, but I suspect you understand quite well the trouble you will bring if you go against us. We are not afraid of the Hulls, so we are certainly not afraid of you."

Without another word, Leon helped Mother Hope to her feet and escorted her out of the trailer.

Max watched as they drove off and wondered what they would say if they knew that Cecily Hull would be arriving any moment. He didn't like the idea of making enemies out of these people, but they were not going to risk much to save Max and Sandra from the Hulls. Cecily, however, would have reasons to do so — at least, Max hoped to convince her that was true.

Less than a minute later, Cecily Hull arrived. She walked in without a word and took a seat, snapping out a cigarette and lighting up. As she blew out smoke, she looked at Max and waited.

"Hello to you, too," Max said. Cecily did not acknowledge his sarcasm. "Okay, then. I guess you'd prefer I be direct."

"And succinct. I don't like to deal with people who've turned me down once before. Makes them hard to trust."

Sandra and Drummond stood in the kitchen and watched the events unfold. Max would have preferred having Sandra by his side — heck, he would have preferred having Sandra run the whole thing — but Sandra said that Cecily would be more amenable with her appearing less important.

Max cleared his throat. "I suppose I should be glad you bothered to come at all."

"Really, Mr. Porter? You think I don't know what went on at Baxter House? Do you honestly believe I wouldn't find out that Tucker failed to get the chest and that you claimed to have located it? That is the only reason I came here. So, do you have it or don't you? Because unless you possess the chest right now,

I have no use for you."

"Four hundred thousand dollars — that's my price." Max tried not to shake when he said the number, but he heard a tiny tremble anyway.

"Aren't you a greedy one?"

"Not at all. My partners want me to get a full million."

Drummond said, "You got that right."

Cecily looked over at Sandra, and Max wondered if she could see Drummond. "Why the discount? I doubt you are simply being nice to me."

Max said, "Four hundred thousand buys us a new house, a new car, and plenty left over to save so we don't have to be under a Hull thumb ever again. But we want more than that. We want your word that you will cease all targeting of me, Sandra, and Drummond — and if you succeed in taking over the Hull family, you will continue to make sure that the three of us are not bothered by you or your people."

Cecily dragged long on her cigarette before giving Max one curt nod.

With that, Max stepped outside to retrieve a sports bag from the trunk of his car. He returned and placed the bag at Cecily's feet. He unzipped it and showed that it was filled with splintered pieces of wood.

"And what is this?" she asked, a dark tone growling beneath her calm voice.

"This is what's left of the chest. After my breakfast, I went back to Baxter House to get it. When Cal Baxter hid the remaining gold under the floorboards of the bottom-most room, he drew a magic circle on the floor. The boards within that circle were made with wood from the chest. That's one reason the circle was so darn powerful and did such a good job of holding McShay against his will."

"He bound McShay to this wood."

"Exactly. And now that Tucker has destroyed McShay, this wood is no longer cursed by a binding spell. But it still holds plenty of magic."

Cecily zipped the bag closed and picked it up. "You have my

word. You, your wife, and your ghost will be free from the Hulls. You will hear from my people in a few days to arrange the payment of your funds."

Drummond flew close in. "Don't let her leave with that bag. We'll never get the money."

Max blocked the doorway. "I want to be perfectly clear. You are welcome to take the bag today because I have no doubts that you will pay up. If you don't, the ghost of Marshall Drummond will come after you."

Drummond passed through Cecily. The chill within her body registered on her face, and Max knew she got the message.

"No need for threats," she said. "You'll be paid."

She motioned to leave, but Max did not move out of her way. "One last thing," he said.

"I'm losing my patience."

"I need you to promise that you will destroy Tucker Hull. All your money, your word — our deal means nothing if I spend the rest of my life worrying that Tucker is going to exact revenge on me at any moment. I've given you this chest so that you can do as you said you wanted to do — destroy him and take over the family."

Cecily dropped her cigarette on the floor. She stepped on it, pressing it in deep. "That is exactly what I will do."

As she left, no one said another word. Max stood by the door long after her car had vanished from sight. He knew he had made a frightening deal — but it was better than no deal at all.

Clapping his hands together in one sharp hit, he turned around, picked up an empty box and started packing. Sandra kissed his cheek and joined in.

Afterword

Thanks for reading Southern Gothic. I hope you enjoyed it as much as, if not more than, the previous books in the series.

One of my great pleasures in writing the Max Porter books is finding all the little odd bits of history to incorporate into the story. This book had quite a few. Among the big ones — the missing shipment of Civil War gold actually happened. People still go along the tracks where Company Shops once existed, hoping to find a coin or two that nobody else has scampered away with. The murder of Chicken Stephens is also true. If you want to know more about him and the chaos of the Reconstruction, check out *Murder in the Courthouse* by Jim Wise. Finally, and biggest of all, the life of O. Henry was as colorful as depicted here — more so, probably. He did live an aimless life, he was indicted for embezzlement, he did run off to Honduras, and he did return for his wife, resulting in his incarceration.

Many of the locations and buildings are real such as the O. Henry hotel, the New Garden Friends School, and the big roundhouse in Spencer. Cal Baxter and Baxter House, however, are entirely my creations, as is the short story O. Henry dedicated to Cal.

About the Author

Stuart Jaffe is the madman behind *The Max Porter Paranormal Mysteries,* the *Nathan K* thrillers, *the Ridnight Mysteries, the Parallel Society* novels, *The Malja Chronicles, The Bluesman, Founders, Real Magic,* and much more. He trained in martial arts for over a decade until a knee injury ended that practice. Now, he plays lead guitar in a local blues band, *The Bootleggers,* and enjoys life on a small farm in rural North Carolina.

For more information, please visit *www.stuartjaffe.com*

www.ingramcontent.com/pod-product-compliance
Lightning Source LLC
Chambersburg PA
CBHW030530310726
48979CB00010B/1867/J

* 9 7 8 1 7 3 3 7 3 0 8 6 0 *